SCRAPPER

PETER J ALDIN

ONE

WITH A FLICK OF MY FINGERS, live video appeared on my helmpanel, streamed from an exterior camfeed on the Bigmouth's starboard hull. It showed three of our four scarabs detaching from mooring pegs and boosting away. Seconds later, the single-occupant runabouts appeared outside the cockpit's forward canopy. Trailing one after the other, they slipped toward the blue glow of the comet captured in a stasis field eight hundred meters off my bow.

"Three away," murmured my co-pilot, "one to go." The cockpits in those Lockheed Bigmouths are so small, I could taste Toby Chang's breakfast on the air. Sausage and onions. Again.

I swung my pilot's chair around one-eighty degrees to face the cockpit's rear wall. On Bigmouths, these walls are covered by a bank of monitors. Twenty screens. Twenty camfeeds. Each devoted to a separate aspect of the collect-and-carry shift's operations. The *middle* of a Bigmouth's cockpit is taken up by a safety railing around the ladderwell that drops into the vessel's main passageway. I put my boots up on that railing, knees bent and kept an eye on all our screens at once—and one screen in particular …

A figure bulked out in e-suit and helmet climbed from the hull onto the last of the four scarabs. Moretti. Angelo Moretti. One of two guys I constantly wished wasn't permanently assigned to my shift crew.

You can choose your job, I thought, *but you can't choose your workmates.*

It took Moretti a good ten seconds to climb around and onto the front face of the scarab. These little ore-collectors are essentially a cube—four-by-four-by-four-meters. Hardglass faces all around, with a ceramsteel frame hosting exterior and interior mounts for the attitude-and-guidance jets, the pilot seat, and the three "arms" poking out front. Each scarab's double grabber arms jut forwards from the top of the frame, rigged to carry a secured load above the cabin so the operator can see forwards at all times. The third arm is a cutter, for carving ore or ice. The back face of a scarab is a mating lock for larger ships' airlocks. Each time one of our crew carved a four-tonne tablet out of the ice, they would use their grabbers to drag it up out of the comet, then out of the stasis field and into open space. From there, the tablet would be ferried to the Bigmouth's open-to-vacuum belly and slid into shelves there.

Moretti was hooking an elbow over one of the grabbers now. No tie-cable for safety—Moretti relied on the magnetics in his boots and whatever strength he had in his arms. Tools and spare parts poked haphazardly from a big carry-pouch strapped to his chest, making it look like a giant metal spider had latched onto him. Procedure was to bring along a sled with all that gear inside it—a sled that should also be affixed to one of the top-mounted railings via cable.

I leaned a little closer to the bank of monitors. "God, look at him. Out in the black untethered again."

In the smaller chair beside mine, Toby gave a distracted shrug, making no comment.

Moretti's voice crackled through the cockpit speakers. "Ya know ya mic's on, Griff?"

"I did know that, yeah." A shove against the railing pivoted my chair forward once more.

"So, you wasn't talking 'bout me behind my back?"

"Wasn't worried about you hearin'. Didn't know you understood long words like *untethered*."

"Don't need a cable, girl."

"Yeah ya do. Ever hear of a little thing called SOP?"

"Sure, girl. Tha's something you say when ya buddy comes in the room. *Sop, dude*?"

"You gonna wheel that one out at Open Mic Night?"

"Like to wheel *you* out ..."

I put one hand on the helm controls. "Finish that sentence, ass-breath, and I'll shake you loose and watch ya spin off into the void."

Laughter rasped through the speakers, but it was strained as Moretti got busy. Anchored by one hand, he started detaching his scarab's faulty las-saw. During the journey out here, routine diagnostics had revealed that the station's techs forgot to refit it after last shift. Moretti had taken control of the comms for a full minute after discovering that, telling the Repair-and-Refit Manager just what he thought of her employees. Making another enemy. He had the las-saw off now. Because he hadn't brought the sled, and because he had no room in his pouch for it, he tossed it out into space to allow his free hand to pull out its replacement.

Watching my screen, Toby shook his head in disgust.

I went one better: "That's some expensive littering right there, Moretti."

"Oops. Slipped."

"Funny," I replied, "that's what the doctor said when she dropped you on your head."

He paused his repairs to locate the hull camera and flipped it the bird good and slow. The gesture wasn't all it could be, not with the fat fingers of an e-suit. But the snickering coming out of the speakers told me Moretti was pretty happy with it.

"You ride all your men this way, Glowin' Head?" he asked. "Or just the cute ones like me?"

I sighed.

Glowin' Head.

Glowin' Head Griffin.

That was what guys like Moretti called me around the station. And I'd smile along as if it was the cleverest joke I'd ever heard—because if I gave the slightest hint of how much I hated running a razor over my scalp every couple of days, the ribbing would only increase. Scrappers working out in the far-flung armpits of the galaxy aren't exactly the kindest of people.

"Just start thinking about what you're doing," I told him. "You're making us all look bad."

"Firstly, I don't take orders from girls," he said, voice strained again as he got the replacement unit in position, the toothed circle of a steel ice saw. "Second, stop hackin' watchin' me!"

"Shift-controllers are paid to watch."

"Voyeurs watch," he replied and snapped the new blade into its housing. "And I hate voyeurs. Little enough privacy out here as is." He applied the nose of a powered wrench to the fitting and tightened the bolts.

"Double check those," I told him. "Don't want it coming loose and cuttin' you in half. Then there'd be two of you, and one's bad enough."

"Stop riding me, Glowin' Head!"

I leaned back in my chair and slid a palm over my head, freshly shaved that morning. While I hated the nickname—and the look—it always surprised me how much I loved the feel of it. The sensation instantly transported me back in time, my smooth scalp reminding me of the river pebbles decorating my childhood bedroom shelves. It was as if I knew I'd be working out around big rocks—asteroids—one day. Some of my pebbles had been fist-sized, some as large as my now-shaven head, others as small as a knuckle—each pebble sourced from a different continent on different colonized worlds. God, I loved those cool, polished rocks: back then I'd never heard terms like "mindfulness" or "coping mechanism". But that's what touching them had been for childhood me. A coping mechanism. For a little girl whose father lived a dangerous life. Whose father was a dangerous man.

That thought snapped me out of the memory, moving my hand from my scalp to the chair's armrests. Questions replaced the images of that old bedroom: *What's making me revert to a childhood coping mechanism? What's got me rubbing my bald head like a touchstone? Moretti?* No, it wasn't him. Truth was, I was used to his carelessness. Everyone was.

He'd survived this long being stupid—it obviously worked for him.

The more likely cause of my unease was the continued silence of the guy seated to my left. Toby Chang had started work at The Sandwich (which is what we called Angelview Station) the same week I did. We'd worked the same shift since, played in the same futsal team every week, eaten the occasional dinner together.

But yesterday had been the day he'd tried for something new; yesterday had been the day he'd asked me out.

I'd turned him down.

And today, things were awkward.

I turned my head and caught him staring.

He covered it by switching his gaze to the screen with Moretti on it. But telltale spots of red on both his cheeks attested to me catching him at it.

I caught my hand rubbing my head again.

Sheesh.

I still missed the silky, black Rapunzel hair of my adolescence. Missed it bad. But when you're on the run, you gotta make sacrifices. I couldn't afford attachments. The whole bald woman thing seemed to be a turn off for most men, especially men I disliked in turn. Imbeciles like Moretti, who thought it hilarious.

Sadly, *not* men like the Tobester.

I straightened in my chair. We had to move past this. We had to work together. Which meant we had to communicate. I told him, "Check the shift order and tell me how many tonnes Management want from that comet today."

On-screen, Moretti had his tools away and was climbing toward the scarab's top evac hatch—a hinged square in the glass meant for emergencies only. *Of course, he is*, I thought. *Why would he do something rational like return to ship, stow the tools and e-suit properly and enter the scarab through the airlock?*

Toby wified his slim to the onboard, flicking through files. "Four hundred fifty." He reported the quota with a note of disgust.

I shared that emotion. Four hundred and fifty tonnes of water ice and rock for four little scarabs to cut and carry in a seven-hour shift? Moretti was going to love hearing he was further behind than he already thought he was ...

"Last week's quotas were three-ninety," I said. "What's Management's hurry? The comet'll still be here tomorrow."

"Management's hurry? They're greedy, that's their hurry. Us little guys keep meeting their quotas, then they punish us by upping the next day's targets."

I grunted agreement, encouraged that I'd found a topic to get him talking again, shift things back toward normal. "Which means if these guys don't work quicker, they have to work longer. Bloody hell. Why the hell not give us an extra scarab? You could run the ship and I could get out there and help them."

He pointed off to our port, toward what looked like a handful of gravel strewn across space. In reality, it was a swarm of asteroids, some larger than our home station. "Coz they're all in there gathering the good stuff. The iridium. The rhodium ..."

I nodded. While those asteroids held precious metals, this comet contained nothing of the sort. Water ice, a little methane, and a lot of dirt. As Moretti got inside his collector, I zoomed my helm camfeed in for a closer view of the comet and its blue aura created by the stasis generators. "Whoever decided to waste power capturing that's probably still rubbing their ass from the kicking. The real reason they're hurrying us is to get it over and done with." I too pointed to the distant asteroid swarm. "That's where they really want us."

He stretched and yawned. "Never know. Might be something valuable in the ice ball. Might be organic materials, frozen in time."

"Organic? So, frozen meals, you mean."

He laughed at that.

I turned my chair around again, put my boots on the ladderwell safety railing and watched the activity on the feeds. This left Toby free to feign busyness with his slim while watching me over the top of it.

Never going to happen, Mr Chang. May as well accept that and move on.

I shifted attention to the three box-jockeys who'd left earlier. Their scarabs had already made cometfall, now busy slicing up eight-cubic-meter chunks ready to ferry into the Bigmouth's belly bay. Twelve of the twenty rear-wall feeds came from the four scarabs. Each collector had three cameras: nose-cams, ass-cams and the interior cab-cams. Moretti's cab-cam showed him wrestling tools in the space behind his seat while working the seals on his helmet. The scarab's diagnostic reported cabin pressure at survivable levels rather than ideal. When he'd tossed the helmet in with the tool pouch, he saluted me through the camera.

"Gonna watch me undress later?" he asked, patting his suit. "Ya forget what I said about voyeurs?"

Spinning around one more time, I thumbed my helm-panel cam on and fed it to his helm monitor. When he noticed me on it, I smiled sweetly and offered him *my* middle finger. Then I cut video to him and audio from him, leaving our cockpit in relative peace.

"He's such an asshole," Toby said.

Yeah, he is, I thought and studied the velvet black of the void outside our ship a moment. *But there's worse people out there. Much worse.*

After Moretti's scarab detached and accelerated away from us, I fired up my own attitude jets. Despite the man's hatred of people watching over his shoulder, I intended to watch over his shoulder. Partly to keep my mind occupied. Partly to piss him off. Nudging the Bigmouth to a higher angle allowed it direct line-of-site to the area he was headed for. All four operators had been assigned an area that the previous shift had turned into a shallow valley. For safety reasons, they worked allotments fifty meters away from each other. The tiny flares from his guidance jets grew tinier, then merged into the glow created the stasis field generators holding the captured comet. I nudged the Bigmouth a hundred meters closer, braking us in full view of the open cut mine, zooming our own nose-cam in on the area.

"Let's see if dumbass takes the allotment I gave him."

"Betcha twenty he doesn't," Toby said with a grin. It was a boyish smile complete with dimples.

"No bet," I said. "But I'll take odds on *how far* he works from the coordinates he's got."

"You're on. Twenty says he'll set down a long way out."

"Wants to make a point, ya think? I reckon the opposite: he'll be out just enough to annoy me without making a big deal. I'll say he's *under* ten metres off-allotment. Anything over that, you win. And let's make it fifty."

"You'll regret that, but, deal," he said and held out a hand.

I slapped it. "Eyes on panel."

He ran his fingers around his sensor feeds. "He's angling in ... and actually approaching at a sane person's speed."

"Yeah, he's only dumb when he thinks we're watching him." I zoomed in on Moretti with our nose cam. "If only he knew."

"He will know. When he makes his first trip back, he'll see us sitting up here."

"I'll drop back down again. Pretend I wasn't snooping."

I cycled through Moretti's three camfeeds on my panel, marking his guidance-jets firing to finesse his approach and perfect his angles. On *his* camera feed, his scarab's grabber-arms reached wide into *spread-eagle* position, staying out of the way so the cutter arm could get busy. The ore-collector lowered itself to face the comet's surface.

Toby's attention was now on his panel. He groaned.

"Distance?" I asked, with a grin of my own. He muttered something. I put a hand to my ear. "Whassat?"

"Eight meters."

"Sweet baby muskpig!" I barked, using Thesian celebratory slang. Always good in the small moments to stay true to the identity you've constructed. I pulled my slim from a thigh pocket and angled it his way. "Make it twenty. I'm nothing if not magnanimous in victory."

Pouting, he tapped on his device. "*Magnanimous.* What the hell kinda word is that?"

I winced a little, realizing my slip. Uneducated Thesians like I was pretending to be didn't speak like that. "Heard it on a streamie. And now you're sour coz I took your money *and* I know more words'n you."

He leaned his slim to mine. Both blipped as the transfer took place. He started to say something but was interrupted by a notification from the helm. A red flag. I checked it, checked a scarab sensor then flipped transmissions back to Moretti's nose-cam. The feed was foggy with ejecta as his ice saw cut deep.

"Oh, crap." I tapped comms. "Moretti, check your tells! Pull your blade."

Toby bent over his own panel. "Christ! He's above a rock vein."

I'd already seen it. "Moretti!"

"Mind your beehive," he muttered from his cab.

"Pull your blade, you goddamned idiot. Pull it and shift one meter starboard before starting again."

On screen, his cutter arm continued tossing up a haze of ice crystals. He said, "Told ya before, newbie girls don't tell me what—"

"You're centimeters from hard rock, Moretti! Pull it *now*."

Ice crystals continued spewing up into the camera's eye. Our other box-monkeys were comming queries at us now, hearing the chatter.

Moretti said, "I know what I'm ..."

His signal cut off abruptly. Simultaneously, we lost the feed from his three cams.

Another scarab pilot swore over the comms. As did Toby. As did I. The other two chattered observations, reports on what they were seeing. On our bridge monitors, their cams caught fragments of the scene—and fragments of Moretti's vehicle.

I found out later that Moretti didn't die from loss of atmosphere. What killed him was the broken half of his ice saw blade, careening up through his cab. Those blades are not made for the uneven densities and surfaces of rock veins. The blade had hit stone and snapped in half.

Moretti died instantly, the experts said later.

It didn't make me feel any better.

TWO

ALTHOUGH MORETTI'S death cut my ten-hour shift short, the preliminary inquest kept me in the station's Admin Precinct long after we'd brought the Bigmouth back in. We'd left the comet as soon as the retrieval team recovered the busted-up scarab ... and Moretti's body.

By the time I was trudging down the passage toward my crib, I'd been awake for twenty hours and a half. My head pounded with fatigue and shock. My stomach was tight with hunger but also churning with nausea. And my breath caught in my throat each time I flashed back to the moment Moretti's saw blade snapped. All I wanted was some alone-time. My roomie would be in there, of course, so I could only hope he'd be fast asleep, given the late hour.

The door lock recognized my face from three meters out and the partition whisked into the wall. I came to a stop just inside the cabin, swaying. The slight breeze of the door closing behind me felt like safety. As did the automatic snick of the lock.

Watson—my roomie—was awake. Wide awake and not

in bed, standing in front of his cider-press and fermenting tub. It was always tough to predict whether or not he would up and about: unlike me, Watson worked rotating shifts.

Also he wasn't human, so his body clock worked differently.

On seeing me, he waddled through the opening we'd cut between our cabins, greeting me with a tall glass of cider and, of all things, a hug. His long and hairy arms wrapped around my waist and squeezed. I leaned my chin on top of his head, the soft fur tickling my skin. Without a sound, he detached and moved across to my workstation to turn off the intranet newsbite he'd been watching. Not quick enough, however: I'd seen it was about the accident. It was no mystery, then, about how he'd known about it. In view of last night's argument, his kindness *was* a surprise ...

Watson was fifteen years old now—as he'd been telling me, repeatedly. Old enough to go seek his own life, he kept insisting, his own path. *All I need is a cash loan from you plus a certificate of release-and-approval*, he'd said last night.

You're a chimpanzat, I'd told him in return. And in a moment of pure frustration-fueled insensitivity, I'd added, *You'll always have the mind of a thirteen-year-old human and it's a damned dangerous universe out there!*

That was true, of course. Everything I'd said was true. He *was* a chimpanzat—as a chimpanzee zygote, he'd been genetically modified with Centauran hive-rat genes. His intelligence *had* been tested as that of a thirteen-year-old human and according to his original owners and the Company's local doctors, it would never develop further.

And it *was* a damn dangerous universe out there.

As attested to by the accident I'd witnessed mere hours ago.

God. Moretti. If only—

I shook myself and sipped the cider. Immediately, its sourness threatened to pucker my entire head. I had to force a straight face.

"This is pretty good," I lied. If Watson could be civil, so could I.

He was already retreating through the gap between our cabins, headed for his flight simulator. We'd bought the thing from another scrapper, one week into our stay here: and Watson had been hooked ever since, playing out adolescent dreams of piloting star fighters or drop ships. His cider brewing apparatus took up the space between it and his cot. It smelled like he'd been cooking during the day; there were fresh bottles circling the fermenting pot like Centauran corglings around a mother corg.

I asked him, "Am I drinking new stuff? Or part of that brew you made last month?"

He paused with his back to me. If today had been yesterday, I might have expected an impolite piece of sign language. For now, he chose politeness, diverting to the shelves beside the simulator to grab his slim. He typed a message, hit send, and waited. My slim pinged. I read what he'd sent.

Last month's. Apple and starberry. Good stuff.

"Damn good stuff." More lies. All in the interests of our newfound truce.

He grunted acknowledgement at the compliment, shelved the slim, and climbed into the simulator. Moments later, he'd fired up the cockpit of a fake Lockheed TB70. And I turned away, so it wouldn't remind me of Moretti.

I chugged more cider. Sure, it was terrible, but I was out of wine. And when you're desperate, even bad booze is good booze. Not ready to sit down yet or take a shower, I wandered the edges of my living space, sipping from the bottle, welcoming the slow build of lightheadedness. My side of the combined apartment was not that big: even a slow lap took me a mere twenty seconds.

On the second lap, I lingered over the things I loved, the artefacts I carried from place to place, the belongings that brought me comfort. A couple I'd brought with me when I'd run; the others had been ordered from the hyper once I was a few fake identities down the line. My pile of dog-eared paperbacks had names on the spines like Verne, Louis Stevenson, Conan Doyle, Wells. The paperbacks were pressed between two leather-bound volumes I used as book ends: *Treasure Island* and *The Hound of the Baskervilles.* HG Wells' sad eyes gazed out from his black-and-white portrait that stood in an old-fashioned photo frame beside the books. Above them all, I'd hooked a small print of the cinema poster for an early movie adaptation of *The Time Machine.*

Like the portrait, the movie poster was also framed and I unhooked it from the wall as I checked over my shoulder. My chimpanzat roomie was lost in his own escape from reality, flying his TB70 through simulated space gravel. I turned the poster over. Another glass panel lay across the back and behind it, face up, a printout of a five-year-old email. *The* email.

Ms Denayer. I write to offer news of your acceptance into our Bachelor of English Literature program. The semester commences in September. Please contact us at the details below. Kindest regards, Salvatore Buzyn, Registrar, Grace City University, Centauri.

I held the poster frame in one hand, my bottle in the

other. Rereading this communiqué had been a senseless whim. It gave me zero comfort. In fact, it surfaced the old anger, curling my fingers tighter around my bottle. I put the cider down, turned the poster around and re-hooked it.

If only Daddy Dearest had allowed me to chase my dream, my simple dream, I thought. *I'd be in Grace City, not this dump. My name would still be Shelby Denayer, not goddamn Jackie Griffin. I'd have all my hair. I wouldn't be working with my hands and my back, but with my mind.*

I wouldn't have seen Moretti die.

I shook my head to clear it of such thoughts, shifting attention to the photographs placed one each side of the poster. To the left, a ten-year-old Shelby Denayer read Jules Verne to a doll upon her lap. To the other, the view from our home when I was fifteen: Daddy's hideout on Foucault's Moon, the lake an improbable shade of blue, the mountain behind it a finger pointing to heaven, the whole thing like a scene from old Earth Canada. Both images had been taken by one of Dad's mistresses, the women I'd grown up calling Aunties.

Tired of this grand tour of someone else's life, I gulped down half the remainder of the cider and tipped the rest into the refresher, rinsing the bottle in the sink. I had a buzz going now, numbing my thoughts, calming them. Since Watson had only an intellectual concept of nudity, I shucked off boots and coveralls, socks and t-shirt, tossing them beside my cot. Off came my bra and on came a clean tee. Clad only in that and undies, I picked out the paperback of HG Wells' *The Invisible Man* and sank into my armchair.

Invisible Man was not one of Wells' better tales, in my opinion. In fact, it was an outright stinker. But immersing myself in it meant not thinking, not hearing Moretti saying *I know what I'm ...* before his signal went dead. Not thinking back over the inquest and the way the reviewer tried twisting my words and wrongfooting me. Maybe an hour of Victorian Era pulp fiction would give me some peace.

I'd read just one paragraph when the door chimed.

I snarled an obscenity at the universe. "Door, who is it?"

The screen above it came to life, depicting a downward view of Toby Chang in the passageway. He held a six-pack of lagers with one hand while the other steadied him against the wall. He squinted up at the cam. "Lemme in, Griff?"

No one came in my cabin.

No one.

Not a janitor. Not a plumber. Not an electrician. And certainly not a drunken workmate.

I tossed *Invisible Man* onto the pile of my clothing. "Door, speaker on. Toby, piss off."

Brightening at the sound of my voice, he stepped away from the wall, swaying uncertainly. A hopeful smile grew across his face. "Open up, Griff? I have booze."

"Who doesn't? Now, go to your own crib and drink yours there. It's late."

"Oh, don't be like that, Griff." He stepped forward and swung the arm with the lagers at the door. I'm sure he intended to do it gently, but it banged hard against it, loud enough for Watson to murmur a wordless question from beneath his immersive-helmet.

"Do that again and I'll kick your butt from here to the nearest airlock!" I yelled at Toby.

"Just let me in for one drink, Griff."

"No."

"Then open the door, Griff, and I'll leave you one drink."

I hesitated. That actually sounded reasonable. The beer

couldn't be worse than Watson's cider. And if it would get rid of him faster ...

I said, "Wait a minute" and drew my coveralls back on before telling the door to open.

The door slid back to reveal his puppy dog eyes and an *I'm-really-not-drunk* tilt of the head. He leaned inside—then started falling and had to stagger forward to catch himself against my breakfast table. As if nothing had happened, he swung the six-pack up and onto it, landing it with a bang. The noise prompted another interrogatory exclamation from Watson in the simulator.

"You and I got something in common, Griff," he said, slurring most of the words.

"Stop ending every sentence with my name."

"I like your name, Griff. And what we have in common, in case you're wondering, and I'm sure you are wondering, is that both of us were trumacized ... turmatized ... messed up—by a bad happening thing. Bad thing happening."

"Yes, we were. So, leave me a beer and get the fleg out." I softened my tone a little. "Try and get some sleep. Like I should be doing."

He pointed a finger at me, narrowing one eye. I'm sure the crooked angle of his smile was meant to look winsome. It didn't. It looked drunk. He said, "You need beer. But you need company too. I know you do. I you know you know you do."

"Tell ya what I need, mister." His eyes opened wide, hopeful. "I need you to *leave my crib and go to yours.*"

He lowered his head, but not in defeat. He was regrouping, thinking, his pickled self-assurance unrattled.

I was exhausted, I was angry, and I started toward him

intending to drive him outside. Before I could reach him, Watson did, appearing out of nowhere.

He rounded Toby, grasped his coveralls by the loose fabric at the hips and swung him straight out the cabin door. Toby found himself running into the passage wall opposite. He whirled, eyes and mouth wide in shock, and staggered toward the door again. Watson barred it with his body—he wasn't tall, but he was broad. Toby hesitated for only a moment, then he tried to push past. Watson swung one arm into the passage. I heard the *crack* of his open palm across Toby's cheek and winced. The Tobester spun one-eighty, Watson kicked him in the ass, and he hit the wall a second time before sliding down it.

It was tough to say what surprised me more. That Watson had performed violence for the first time ever. Or that he'd done it with such calm, precision, and control. I came to his shoulder and looked down at his hands as they busily formed a statement for Toby in sign language.

"Watson says, 'Nobody comes into our crib'."

"Flegging hell," Toby moaned.

"Now, go home, Toby. And thanks for the beer." I was about to pull Watson inside and tell the door to lock, but Watson had his own ideas. He stomped out into the corridor and reached down for Toby. I had a heart-lurching moment when I thought he was going to hit him again—but Watson simply dragged him to his feet, laced one of the man's arms over his shoulders and began walking him back down the passage toward Toby's apartment fifty meters away.

I dumped my ass on my bunk and put my head in my hands, mind whirling again. *What the hell was that?* Watson had never done that before. Had it been the loud noises, startling him? Some hive-rat *defend-the-nest* instinct kicking in? One friend angrily protecting another?

The door slid shut and locked, making me look up. Avoiding eye contact, Watson stepped to the table, plucked the six-pack from the table and carried it to the cooler.

"Honey, that was amazing," I said.

He shrugged and closed the cooler.

"You're the best friend I've ever had."

He glanced at me, face like stone, then moved across to his slim. He preferred it to sign language when what he wanted to say was more complex or nuanced. Or when he wanted the words to linger there on my screen for maximum impact. He typed something, and returned to his simulator.

I bent over my device and read the words he'd sent. My mood plunged.

Watson had written, *If we're such good friends, why won't you let me go live my own life?*

THREE

Management gave me the next day off. A psych day, they called it.

This coincided with Watson's regular rest day—we all received one of these every six days—and that left me with a choice. I could mope around a confined space while The Grumpy One also moped around the same confined space; or I could head out to the shopping precinct. Pretty easy decision.

At around 1100 hours, I made myself clean and presentable, picked up my newly arrived antique copy of Conan Doyle's *Tales of Terror and Mystery* and headed out to the door. Watson lay on his cot, his nose in a paper comic about a part-ape part-human superhero. Since he was ignoring me, I left without saying goodbye.

When designing Angelview Station, the Company had made the public areas wider than they needed to be, perhaps to relieve long term spacers from the claustrophobia of small cabins and small ship spaces. The

Concourse—our shopping precinct—was the best of these, and a ten-minute wander from my door.

Bissouma-Douglas's Angelview Station was comprised of three colossal modules. We called 'em *Slices*, because the station really did look like a giant sandwich from the outside.

Top Slice: Recreation/Infrastructure Module. Gym and sporting facilities. Security offices. Maintenance department. Storage.

Middle Slice: Logistics/Operation Module. The warehouse. East Hangar and West Hangar (the directions nominal of course since there's no direction in space). Ore/ice cleaning: the small area between West Hangar and the warehouse proper, where the chunks brought in by Bigmouths were partly refined before being repackaged for storage.

Bottom Slice: Commercial/Residential/Administration Module (Yes: CRAM. Someone didn't think that one through). A module split "north"-to-"south" into three zones, three strips. The accommodation precinct taking up the western quarter, admin taking up the eastern one, with the Concourse dominating the middle.

The Slices were a kilometer each side.

A small dome was fixed above the Top Slice and another below the bottom, supplemental modules housing things like the FTL comms-transmitters, in-system radio/laser transmitters, sensor arrays, backup servers, meteoroid defenses, etc. Whoever had come up with The Sandwich-based nicknames for things had dubbed the top dome the Olive. But the bottom one? That was where the metaphor fell apart. They'd called that the Hemorrhoid.

I know.

The route I chose to walk brought me out dead center of the long mall, emerging between Jonjo's Hydroponics Supplies and the Running Shoe Emporium, and opposite the Two Cousins hookah lounge. That's hook*ah*, not hook*er*: while a little recreational hashish was okay as long as a worker took legal stims to counter it while on-shift, the Company's *People and Policy* department would never have approved of prostitution. Or of harder drugs than hashish. Staring at Two Cousins—which was teeming—I rubbed at my achy temples and wondered if they shouldn't ban drinking multiple bottles of Martian beer also. I'd paused mindlessly in the entryway and a passerby brushed my shoulder, startling me into motion again.

Two doors up from the hookah lounge sat the tea house I frequented, a quaint little venue whose décor fused Modern Caultan with Victorian English. I stepped through an arched entryway framed with stained-glass into faux yellow gaslight and lavender-flavored air. In the corner to my left, a hologram of a waist-coated man played Gilbert & Sullivan's *A Wandering Minstrel* on the piano-forte. The small café was devoid of other customers, so I stood there a moment with eyes closed, savoring the air, savoring the sound, savoring the solitude. Feeling the weight of the universe slide off my shoulders. Even my head stopped pounding so hard.

"Hellowhatdoyouwant?"

The sudden intrusion of the voice jarred me, snapping my eyelids open. Proprietor Jamie Dubois stood in the kitchen entry wiping his hands on a dish cloth. Jamie was an okay guy, pretty purple irises, gold-tinted skin, sea-horse tatts on both forearms. He ran a clean restaurant, made a mean cucumber sandwich, brewed a perfect tea. But although I came in here two or three times a week, he never once remembered my name. Or my order. And he'd never heard of the concept of friendly service.

"Hello, Jamie," I said.

"Hello." He waited. The dish cloth worked between his fingers.

"Three macaroons, any flavor. Cucumber sandwiches. Pot of English breakfast tea, strong, and a decanter of cow's milk." Same as always.

"Surefindaseat." He vanished into the kitchen. The tea room's ambience was relaxing ... except for its manic owner.

"Find a seat," I deadpanned to the holographic piano-player. "That'll be difficult."

I settled into the booth in the furthest corner from the door, a habit no doubt gleaned from my father. I donned cloth gloves—something Jamie wouldn't even notice, let alone laugh at—and opened my new Conan Doyle hard-back. I read the first paragraph of *The Horror of the Heights* ...

The idea that the extraordinary narrative which has been called the Joyce-Armstrong Fragment is an elaborate practical joke evolved by some unknown person, cursed by a perverted and sinister sense of humor, has now been abandoned by all who have examined the matter. The most macabre and imaginative of plotters would hesitate before linking his morbid fancies with the unquestioned and tragic facts which reinforce the statement. Though the assertions contained in it are amazing and even monstrous, it is none the less forcing itself upon the general intelligence that they are true, and that we must readjust our ideas to the new situation. This world of ours appears to be separated by a slight and precarious margin of safety from a most singular and unexpected danger.

I leaned back, let the book cover close and sighed. I sighed twice. First, from the pure delight I always experienced at the Englishman's ostentatious and over-cooked prose. Second, at the note of resonance I'd found in the last line of that paragraph. *This world of ours appears to be separated by a slight and precarious margin of safety from a most singular and unexpected danger.* Didn't I know it? I knew that very well.

My tea arrived. And my macaroons.

"Sandwichescoming," Jamie announced before zooming away. He zipped around tables and chairs the way ... the way Moretti's scarab used to zip around space rocks and debris.

Another sigh. I let the tea steep. I nibbled an orange-flavored macaroon and threw myself back into *The Horror*. When I was twelve years old, I'd been reading an old book like this, *The Island of Doctor Moreau*, and Daddy had seen me reading it, asked me what it was about. Probably, he'd been irritated that my attention was on it and not him. He'd puffed out his chest while saying, "Gennied animals? I can buy you a few if you want." (Which was code, I later deduced, for *steal you a few*). I'd said no thanks, which deflated him a little, but at that stage I'd been happier with the fantasy inside a book rather than making my physical world any more ... exotic.

Nine years later, on the run and creating my own kind of fantasy, I'd come across Watson for sale on a corporate netsite. Gennied animals like chimpanzats had just become commercially available, used mainly for manual labor jobs where companies didn't trust robots but couldn't afford the legal liability toward humans. He'd looked so cute in the photo that I couldn't stand the idea of him becoming someone's slave. And though it cost me fully half the funds I'd stolen from Daddy Dearest, I'd purchased him, calling him my companion from then on when anyone asked, claiming he'd been left to me in a rich Uncle's will.

He'd been smart enough to accept that this lie worked in his interest, providing him a modicum of freedom within the cautious lifestyle we shared. Eventually, I'd trusted him with my backstory also. Because a chimpanzat was a curiosity, but not really a remarkable sight within the kinds of remote industries I worked in, I felt comfortable having him with me without him being a clue for Daddy's fixers to find me.

At Angelview Station, Watson had been offered work as an assistant on a garbage skiff. It was at half-salary—that salary paid into my account on his behalf—but it was also a huge step up from the duties a chimpanzat might have expected here, such as crawling through sampling holes in asteroids to retrieve broken drill bits or planting explosives.

I blinked out of my reverie, finding I'd turned three pages I had no memory of reading. Also, the sandwiches had arrived unnoticed.

I poured tea for myself, added a splash of milk and two teaspoons from a brown sugar canister. Finally, I began to relax, to focus on the book. I was nearing the end of *The Horror* short story—and the end of my first cup of tea—when two scrappers in rest-day clothes barged through the entry, bumped and thumped their way across the room and dumped themselves in the next booth.

Do you mind! I thought, glowering at them.

Oblivious to the way they were disturbing me, they traded vulgar insults before guffawing and slapping each other's backs like Watson's ancestors. (Ok, like my ancestors too). When Jamie appeared, they yelled across to him for "two big iced chocolates and four serves of mud cake, with fritterbug nuggets as sides".

Presumably, no one had ever told them that fritterbugs were neither Caultan nor English as befitted the teahouse's theme; they were, in fact, Centauran. Returning to their conversation, neither saw Jamie roll his eyes before he returned to his kitchen.

The two men continued to yack raucously. The words blurred on my page. My cucumber sandwiches lost their flavor.

Gimme a hacking break, I grumbled, allowing my Thesian identity to take control of my thoughts for a moment. *There's twelve other booths and tables here and you gotta pick that one?*

With a jolt, I realized something. Four years ago, even two, I'd have been immediately suspicious of these two. I'd have wondered if they were private investigators or bounty hunters, placed there to check me out. The fact that the idea came to me so slowly now turned my irritation inward. *What was that quote you used to repeat on a loop?* I scolded myself. *Something about eternal vigilance being the price of liberty?*

The side-eye I'd been giving them changed in focus from resentment to scrutiny. I didn't know the men. They weren't showing me any interest, and that might have been due to the bald head. It might also have been due to them being good at bounty hunting. Both had laid their slims on the table, comparing photos they'd taken of a "leafy green" ship up in East Hangar, *leafy green* being a local colloquialism for wonderful.

"Dart class," one said.

"Nope, definitely StarJumper class," said the other.

"Yeah, ok, maybe. Looks like the Hellfish model from this angle, so maybe."

As they moved onto discussing specs and techs, I got out my slim and took a sneaky photo of my own. Running their faces through my hack into the station's People and Policy files told me they were legit. Just run-of-the-mill clueless morons. Moron #1 had been on-station for four months and Moron #2 for three. A little less than me, but no bounty hunter was going to hang around here that long. Relaxing, I put my slim away and popped the rest of a sandwich into my mouth. On one of their screens, I caught sight of the ship they were discussing: a svelte personal cruiser normally used by arrogant rich kids, not on-duty Company executives or health-and-safety inspectors.

My neighbors' shakes arrived and they changed topics again ...

"Chocolate is the greatest thing we ever invented."

"No, it isn't, it's the wheel."

"You can't eat a wheel, idiot."

"You can't make chocolate without wheels, idiot."

It became clear I wouldn't be getting any peace here. I scarfed the rest of my sandwiches, pocketed my final macaroon and stood to leave. Maybe I'd go shopping for garbage I didn't need. Or aspirin. Better yet, I could head into the admin precinct and see if Chaplain Montez had made plans for Moretti's memorial ceremony.

I caught a last glimpse of the Hellfish cruiser as I passed

the morons' table. It was a beaut, all right. Leased-to-impress by some exec or sales rep no doubt.

At the door, I put my finger to my forehead in a polite salute to Jamie Dubois. He shrugged back. I was sure that, when next I saw him, he'd have forgotten me entirely. Again. But after the scare with the Morons, I realized that wasn't so bad. After all, I *wanted* people to forget me.

FOUR

WHAT SADIST DESIGNED THIS PLACE?

Tea and cucumber churned in my stomach as I entered admin precinct and glanced both ways along it. The sector was half as wide as the Concourse and lacked any of the shopping zone's sexiness. In fact, it was as if someone had done the following ...

First, they'd asked, "How can we make this precinct vibrant, in a way that makes people want to visit and do their work with a song in their heart?"

Next, they'd collected the best advice on that subject.

And finally, they'd gone and done the exact *opposite*.

Burnt orange carpet ran the full nine hundred meters. On the arterial passageway's floor. Also, along its ceiling. Why the designers had carpeted the ceiling was a constant topic of debate among bored scrappers. The walls were a dusty blue; but wherever there was a seam between the steel plates, someone had painted a lime green stripe over the welding. Lilac-and-bronze striped bench seats had been conveniently placed along the thoroughfare at ten meter-intervals ... as if anyone would want to sit here and take their lunch, or sit here at all. Although it was close to lunchtime, not a soul rested on any of the benches. No one stood outside offices, chatting. Two people in the distance hurried across from one office to another, as if the carpet was hot to walk on.

I'd come in halfway along the arterial and the Chaplain's office was a one-hundred-meter walk to my left. I hastened across putrid-colored deep shag pile, hurrying past silk wall hangings of purple waterfalls, veering around a water feature with a Centauran hive-rat spewing frothing blue liquid from his mouth.

Not soon enough, I arrived at the sign that said *Chaplaincy*.

I paused. Across the way and maybe ten meters along was another sign: *CHIEF OPERATIONS OFFICER*. It glowed in neon from above a wide office window. Directly behind that window lay, of course, the COO's *assistant's* desk rather than the COO's; no one was going to barge in on that pot-bellied scarecrow unannounced. Hyram Craig had attended yesterday's inquest for a good half hour, leveling filthy looks at me while I was grilled.

Up close, I saw there was a second notice on the chaplain's door, this one a small hologram protruding from it in dark lettering. *COUNSELING IN SESSION — DO NOT DISTURB*.

Well, that was okay, I had nothing better to do than wait —in a cruelly decorated corridor trying its hardest to reignite my headache. And succeeding. As I sank down on the bench outside Chaplaincy, I could only hope that Hyram Craig wouldn't come out of his office now, wouldn't see me.

At that exact moment, his office door opened.

I got half my wish.

He didn't see me.

But he did come out of his office.

And if that wasn't enough to freeze my heart in my chest, then the sight of the guy who came out with him was.

I'd been thinking of Daddy's goons only ten minutes earlier in Jamie Dubois' tea room. And here—just ten meters away—here, was one of them. The *worst* of them. Dressed in an even more expensive suit than the COO's. His hair slicked into a short ponytail.

Scuttle!

A dumb name for a relentless, crafty, soulless monster.

The man who'd been my father's go-to fixer kept pace with Craig as they strolled away in the opposite direction from where I sat. His ponytail bobbed and swung lazily as the second-worst man I'd ever known walked along, chatting amiably with Craig.

I curled over on my seat. Choices. I *had* choices. I could turn and hurry off the other way; if he looked back, he wouldn't see Shelby Denayer, just a bald woman in cheap active-wear. But if he saw me here, glued to this bench, staring after him—hair or no hair, he'd know me. And yet I was glued to the seat, unable to tear my eyes away from the back of his head.

Scuttle!

I hissed, "What the *hack* is he doing here?"

Was he working for another crew now? Could he have left Daddy Dearest? And lived? Or had he gone legit? He sure looked like a sales rep in that gray suit, with that slicked hair.

They were twenty meters away now. And then they were

thirty. Forty. Possibly headed for the exclusive management bar-and-grill up that way. At any moment he might say "Oh, I left my wallet in your office!" And turn back. And see me.

I finally broke my freeze, and leapt up and pushed through the closest door, poking the edge of my face around the jamb so I could watch them saunter the final sixty meters to the bar. Sweat dampened my armpits. My lungs turned to steel; they wouldn't let me get enough air. Bile burned the back of my throat.

How can...? What is he...?

"Excuse me!" someone barked behind me.

I turned my head. Not enough to look. Enough to say, "Sh!"

"Don't *sh* me!" the deep voice said, rising in volume.

"All right, shut up then," I told whoever it was. Scuttle and Craig were seconds away from the bar. If that's where they were headed. I could break cover when they were inside.

"How dare you!" the voice behind me growled.

But what if they weren't going to the bar? They might be going for the personnel lifts that end of the precinct, going up to the—

Hellfish. It's his!

"Are you listening to me? This is a private session!"

The words registered, but not their meaning. Now Scuttle and Craig had reached the bar. Craig waved Scuttle in ahead of him. When Dad's chief hench-monster was finally out of sight, I sagged, my head against the door frame.

Oh, God. That was so close! He's here for me. He has to be.

But he hadn't seen me. And he was going for a *drink*: no urgency in an act like that.

A second voice—also male—spoke up from within the room at my back. "It's all right, Chaplain, I was done anyway."

My head snapped round as I recognized it. It dawned on me whose office I'd pushed my way into.

On the far side of a room adorned with soothing colors and potted ferns, Toby rose from one of two armchairs. The other chair was occupied by a fuming Chaplain Montez; a notepad sat on the lap of his tan corduroys. One hand clutched a pen like he wanted to stab me with it; the other attempted to wave Toby back to his chair. Toby straightened his shirt and flipped back his long fringe. He gave no sign he intended to sit down.

"Oh," I said. Then, "Shit." Then, "Sorry, Chaplain. I shouldn't swear like that."

"Trust me, I'm thinking far worse swear words than that," he said. "And what you should be apologizing for is bursting in on a private counseling session!" He slapped the pen to the notepad with a loud clap.

My attention turned fully to Toby who stood mid-room, poised as if waiting for me to get out of the way. In the Chaplain's lamplight, a bruise showed plainly across Toby's left cheek. I winced a little: had Watson hit him *that* hard? The little bugger didn't know his own strength apparently.

I said, "You're getting counseling?" Silly thing to say. I was flustered, reeling.

"Yeah." He squeezed his eyes shut a moment. "Can't get it out of my head. Moretti. He was alive one minute. Then ..." He gathered himself, plunged his hands in his pockets, cleared something from his throat. "Is that what you're here for?"

"Me?" My hand went to my breastbone. "I ... No. I ..."

For the life of me, I couldn't remember what I'd come here for. Pounding away at my attention was the fact that one of Dad's henchmen was here on The Sandwich. The *worst* of Dad's henchmen. I took a step out the door and off Montez's firm, gray carpet.

"I'm sorry," I said. With a final glance at Toby, I added, "To both of you."

Then I was hurrying back the way I'd come from. Headed for my cabin. By the time I reached the Concourse, I was running.

———

After one actual collision with shoppers and three near misses, I quit the running. Sprinting through a space station was a sure-fire way to get noticed. And noticed got you caught.

With my head down and my hands in my pockets, I slunk the rest of the way to my rooms, fighting the urge to scream the whole time. My quick entrance startled Watson who was pouring a cup of milk, making him spill it. He was using my kitchen, my cup, my milk. This morning, I'd have scolded him for it; right now, I could care less.

Mopping at the milk on the bench, he made an inter-rogatory grunt. I ignored it, brushing by him to pull the last of Toby's beers from the cooler. My mouth was dry, my thoughts spiraling out of control. I chugged a good third of it before starting to pace my side of the cabin.

The same phrase repeated on a loop within my brain: *whatamIgonnado whatamIgonnado whatamIgonnado ...*

My slim sounded its magpie song, indicating a message from Watson. He'd moved to his side without me noticing. The message said, *What happened to you? You look like crap.*

He'd probably meant it as concern, but my adrenalized brain wasn't reading it that way. Anger boiled up and I typed back: *Up yours.*

I watched through the open doorway as he read it. He turned yellow eyes upon me for a second, gave me a slow headshake, then coolly typed a reply before tossing the slim on the shelf and climbing into his simulator. His message read, *Back at ya, baldie.*

I grumbled something equally insulting at him while swiping his message-window aside. The little bugger better enjoy the simulator as much as he could now, I thought: he wouldn't be bringing it with him when we burn-assed our way out of here.

The thought was unkind, born of fear and frustration. Needing a clear head, I lay the beer down.

For the next ten minutes, I scoured the station's intranet for newsbites of Scuttle's visit, while the nonsense-loop coalesced into clearer thoughts that rolled and bumped within my skull. *Did he see me? Is he here on a job? Is he even with Dad anymore? What did I do, what mistake did I make? Are they looking for me?* That last one was dumb. Of course they were looking for me. It had been four years, sure. But, unless Daddy was dead—and I'd have heard about that if he was, even out here—his crew would never give up. Especially Scuttle.

There was a chance that I wasn't the reason he was here. It might be another job. Also, he might have joined another crew.

I gave up looking for signs of his purpose online. There was nothing in the newsfeed about him or any other visitor.

The only item in the logs I hacked was confirmation that a Hellfish *had* landed two hours back. Obviously, Scuttle was masquerading as some bigwig, so perhaps he was on a con here. I could hope that was the case. But I couldn't rely on it.

"Time to leave," I mumbled, turning my search-focus to Bissouma-Douglas's career page. There had to be vacancies at its dozen other offworld plants and facilities scattered through Corporate Union space. A few of those were like ours: mining and processing and shipping. Others were devoted to one of those tasks alone. One, I knew, was a refueling station our company had the current contract for.

None of them had vacancies. Not. One. Single. Job.

"What the crap!" I said aloud. There'd been talk of a downturn, of company cutbacks. Little did I think the gossip would affect me so directly. So direly.

Then again, if Scuttle had my scent, staying with the Company was probably a bad idea. If they knew of my current Jackie Griffin persona.

Tossing the slim onto my bunk, I looked to my shelves of precious artefacts. To the books, to the poster, to the photograph of HG Wells. I wished for his time machine. *What would your characters do, Mr Wells? In a circumstance like this. Would they flee? If so, to where? And how?*

Fleeing was exactly what I had to do. A job didn't matter. Not in the short term. I had a few kay stashed away, enough to get by while I set up somewhere again with …

I glanced at Watson. Yes, with him. The half-ape, half-alien-rodent.

I'd tried to deny it all these years, to bury the niggling worm of worry at the back of my mind. But anywhere I went, an adult chimpanzat in my company *was* a talking point, a flag of sorts for those looking for me. I glanced again toward him, playing his game, flying his simulated space fighter. My best friend for years had become the guy I argued with almost constantly now. And he had become a liability.

Or was I the liability to him, I wondered suddenly. Was I the obstacle to *his* freedom? I glanced toward the HG Wells books on my pile, first at the *Island of Doctor Moreau*, thinking of the island's trapped and hapless animal hybrids ...

... and then at *The War of the Worlds*. Something made me remember the scene where the narrator-character begins to emerge from his "imprisonment", when the first living creature he comes across is a dog, and how he first sees the dog as potential food! Was my conscience drawing a connection there, creating an awkward metaphor? Had I been so starving for comradeship upon leaving my adolescent imprisonment that I'd snapped up Watson and enslaved him in that role?

You should let him go; give him the freedom he wants.

But if I did that, then I'd be alone.

You selfish little cow.

No, I *wasn't* selfish! I argued with myself, forcing myself to believe it. There was a good reason not to let Watson go, the one I'd appealed to in every argument we'd ever had on the topic. How the hell would an ape-rat with the mind of a 13-year-old human survive in the big wide universe? Without me? Nope, Watson was coming with me.

So. We needed to find some kind of bolt hole. Somewhere to regroup and *think*. Think about the future, of better ways to avoid scrutiny.

Damn it.

It hit me then: we couldn't run today. Running while

Scuttle was here was not an option. It would be noticed. And there were no ships headed out-system today anyway. To get out of this remote and uncolonized system, I'd have to resign my job (give one week's notice), complete paperwork, book a flight on the weekly out-shuttle ...

"Damn *it*."

I was stuck. For now.

Okay, okay. Think it through, I told myself as I leaned back in my chair and took a long deep breath. *If Scuttle knows you're here, wouldn't he be at that door by now?*

"That's a point," I whispered on an exhaled breath. What the hell would he be waiting for?

Grabbing my slim, I checked the station's vehicle tracking page. Then punched the air and whooped. His Hellfish had left station exactly two minutes ago.

I thought of him and Craig entering that bar. *Must've been a quick drink before departure.*

"You're safe," I told myself, still in a whisper. "You're okay, you're safe."

It was a lie and I knew it.

With a father like mine, I wasn't safe.

I never would be.

───────

THE BIG QUESTION REMAINED. WHAT IN EVERY RELIGION'S hell had Scuttle been doing here? I had to know. I *had to*.

Since there was no helpful information online, the quickest way to get it was to ambush Hyram Craig. Which wasn't hard to do, since I knew exactly where he'd be at around 15:00, *and* he'd have no minders to stop me. Because today was Wednesday.

Wednesdays, Craig always went up to the Top Slice for a low-grav racquetball game, starting at 15:15. This weekly event was streamed around the station's intranet for the entertainment of the masses. That's what management said. Two distinct groups tuned in regularly: the sycophants who'd send Craig congratulatory pings for every point he scored against some poorly matched opponent; and bunches of bored, off-shift jokers hosting "Craig Parties" to mock the COO's every clumsy move.

I didn't belong to either. But, like everyone else, I sure knew about the matches.

And so, I waited outside the rec precinct change-rooms at 14:45, in case Craig was early to his warm up. People wandered alone or in pairs both ways along the passageway—maintenance techs, off-shifters heading to the basketball courts or futsal pitches, one security guy who gave me some stink-eye but moved on without comment. I'd brought along a grumbling Watson, knowing Craig had a soft spot for the little guy and would pause to say hello to him. Craig had twice played cards against Watson at "Staff Morale Events", only just winning on both occasions.

Craig had beaten me here. A couple minutes after we arrived, he emerged from the change-rooms looking the part: white polo shirt and shorts, pink tennis shoes, sports bag over one shoulder—even a sweatband circling his head.

I pushed off the wall opposite the door. "Mr Craig, hi!"

"What? Oh." His face fell as he recognized me. "Griffin, is it? Look, if you're trying to find out about the inquest, this is hardly the time nor the method—"

"No, sir. No, no. I'm up here for entertainment and inspiration. Thought I'd sit in the gallery and watch your game."

"Oh? Oh. Well. That's pleasant to hear. Let's hope my game doesn't disappoint."

"It never does, sir. I watch the replays after my shift every Wednesday. Never missed a one."

I hoped he wouldn't call my bluff on that. But like most busy and arrogant men, he accepted that with a nod and a smirk. "Good to hear. Please excuse me. If I don't get a move on, I *will* disappoint."

As he moved by, I fell into step beside him. Watson trailed along behind. I hadn't yet explained our predicament to him. He thought I'd brought him up here to get us a better relationship with the boss and a pay rise.

I said, "Hey, I heard there's a totally zing Hellfish in East Hangar."

"Er ... Oh, yes. Belonged to a sales rep." He made a dismissive motion that ended with him looking at his wristwatch. "Trying to sign us up to a new brand of sewage treatment services. He's left the station now."

"He has? Oh, damn. I didn't get to take a picture of it." He made a noise I'm sure was intended as empathy but which sounded more like the impatient groan of a distracted man. He picked up the pace. With the entry to the courts approaching fast ahead, I asked, "Will he be back? I'd sure like to get a look at that ship."

"No," he said. "No, he won't be back. Now, you must excuse me." He sped up and vanished through the door.

"Knock em dead, sir!" I called after him. Then turned to find Watson shaking his head at me. "What?"

"You're an idiot," he signed.

"And you have a hairy butt," I chuckled, relaxing now I sensed our immediate danger passing. "Shall we get some tea?" Watson liked tea. Also, the milkshakes Jamie Dubois made.

"You don't get it," he signed. "You're an idiot because you think I don't know what's going on."

I made an innocent face.

He pulled out his slim and started typing. I read as it streamed across mine. *You were so distracted at home, you didn't see me walk past while you were looking at records. I saw the security-cam grab you had in the right-hand corner of your screen. That was that Scuttle guy, wasn't it?*

I gulped, hesitated, nodded. Damn his ape curiosity. And my distractedness.

His words were still scrolling. *He was here and you were trying to find out why. Weren't you?*

I swallowed and nodded again.

He abandoned typing, tucking his slim in the back of his pants, and reverted to sign. "Did you think I wouldn't find out? Did you think I shouldn't know?" His hands moved at a blur, his expression dark, teeth bared. I'd really pissed him off this time. "You don't trust me and you think I'm a child. No, you think I'm an animal. I'm sick of you. I hate you."

He ran then, dropping into the loping four-limbed sprint of his chimp progenitors.

I stared after him, grief a lump in my throat where earlier I'd had fear. There'd been civility between us since Moretti's death. I'd just torpedoed it. I glanced the other way, the way Craig had gone, thinking that the good news was Scuttle hadn't seen me and wasn't returning.

"I guess that evens things out?" I wondered out loud.

I wasn't sure it did.

For now, at least, Watson and I were safe. As long as Scuttle really was legit now and not planning some scam that required his return. I couldn't see a reason he'd go legit. And I couldn't take the risk that he wouldn't return.

Sitting in Jamie Dubois' tea room at 16:00, I booked a seat on next Tuesday's out-shuttle. My email to People and Policy demanded personal leave to attend a family wedding. When I didn't return, they'd fire me retrospectively and black-ban me from working in any Bissouma-Douglas subsidiary. Which wouldn't bother me one bit. Because the next time I went looking for work, I'd have a different name. And a different haircut.

I ran a hand over my head.

Maybe I'd try a blonde wig next.

FIVE

THE FOLLOWING MORNING at 06:30, I received notification that the inquest had cleared Toby and me of any negligence. And why wouldn't it, I grumped.

However—there's always a *however*—because I'd been the nominal shift supervisor and because the Company feared psychological consequences from my trauma, I was suspended from off-station (space) tasks for a month. There *were* psychological consequences. I'd seen someone die. But it wasn't the first time. And I would handle it a lot better than most people. Also, no shift supervisor had the power to stop someone like Angelo Moretti from making a mistake.

The inquest also found that Moretti had been under the influence of hashish *and* alcohol while flying. He'd boarded our Bigmouth after somehow dodging the mandatory drug-testing all box-monkeys took. Someone else was going to get spanked over that one ...

Moretti's intoxication led to an indefinite suspension on the recreational use of hashish (which Two Cousins Lounge wasn't going to like). But there was no talk of banning the booze (wise if Management didn't want a riot on their hands).

It also led to an unfortunate consequence for Moretti's family. (*He has a family?* I wondered, more than a little shocked). His wife and children wouldn't receive compensation. The scrapper's life insurance was also in doubt.

That angered me. Okay, Moretti was responsible for being irresponsible. But that was not his family's fault. Over a bowl of cereal in my crib, I hacked his family's details and emailed them an anonymous gift of three thousand dollars to tide them over.

Due to my suspension from off-station duties, Management put me on afternoon shift on the warehouse floor. Suited me fine. It was easy work and safe work, alternating between forklift duties, picking orders and packing orders. The priority was not disputing duty assignments, but keeping my head down and acting normal. Afternoon shift meant less people on the warehouse floor, allowing me to keep to myself.

Also, it further minimized the times when Watson's downtime and mine would coincide. Our running argument had flared up at breakfast when I hinted we might be leaving next week. And I was in no mood for further rounds.

And so, I started the shift at 16:00, feeling good about staying busy, keeping my mind busy, having time to myself.

At 21:30, my work was interrupted.

I was using a stasis-jack to ease a twelve-tonne block of force-field-encased water ice out of its place on the shelves. I stopped when my supervisor yelled at me down the aisle.

"Message for you!" She indicated the commlink in her ear. "Craig wants to see you. Now."

I powered-down the jack and shouted back. "What? Why?"

She raised her arms in an elaborate shrug and moved out of sight.

Oh, God, I thought. *Please, don't let him think I was crushing on him yesterday.*

If there was anything in the universe worse than Scuttle finding me, it would be Craig hitting on me.

I shifted the ice block back into its fixture and left the jack attached but powered down as I trudged down the aisle away from it.

I could only hope whatever Craig wanted wouldn't take long.

And that he'd keep his hands to himself. I couldn't afford to get arrested for breaking them.

As THE LIFT DESCENDED, I WIPED SWEAT FROM MY SCALP AND daydreamed about kickstarting a new identity on a paradise world like Oceana. Maybe I could work on a beach with warm sunshine and cool breezes. When I stepped out again, the time on the lift display was 21:38 and the admin precinct was deserted. Being after hours, the lighting had been muted to save power. I was thankful for this because it took the edge off the horrors of that décor.

I opened the door to Craig's office reception area and stepped inside. I'd never been here before. Though the lights were also low, it was nice compared to the passage outside. To my left, a window ran from floor to ceiling, tinted to make it harder, though not impossible, to peer in from outside—perhaps also to color-shift the appearance of the passage carpet. Roman blinds had been lowered across it. The carpet appeared a cool grey and the walls were hung with tasteful watercolors of various cultures and styles. A long, leather settee sat against the far side wall, while someone had potted a pretty, sweet-scented Oceanean lily by the assistant's desk. The flower reminded me of my elevator daydream of working at an edenic resort on its homeworld. Its petals had sprayed open, inviting inspection by pests—which the lily would then ensnare and ingest. I wondered what they fed it in here.

The inner door to Craig's inner office was open and the light was on. The COO stood at his standing desk, bowed over a large corporate slab with stylus in hand. Behind him, dark wooden bookshelves hosted leather-bound spines of thick hardbacks along with a variety of knickknacks and tiny animated holograms.

Lingering in the outer room, uncomfortable at proceeding further, I distracted myself for a moment wondering if those books were real. Were they, perhaps, a mocked-up veneer created to give the impression of a wealthy and well-read man? If they *were* real, then the bibliophile in me was a little jealous, and really wanted a peek at them. However, no matter what his agenda, I was pretty sure Craig wouldn't let me get anywhere close to them.

Announcing myself with a small cough, I moved past the assistant's desk. Craig straightened and waved me in.

There was a tightness to his face, a weirdness I couldn't read. And I have kicked myself ever since for not listening to my gut about it. Something in my instincts sent up a red flag, but I was so used to seeing threats everywhere, that I dismissed it.

I stepped into his office—and into the rough grips of the people standing either side of the door.

My struggles to break free may as well have been those of a roach trying to escape the Oceanean lily behind me. Those powerful hands and arms had me. I wasn't going anywhere. My breath caught as I recognized the pair.

The one locked onto my left arm was Umesh, a longtime thug employed by Daddy. He looked a little grayer-of-hair than last I'd seen him, but he was obviously still up for the task of abducting women. He wore a suit like I'd seen on Scuttle, but it didn't fit Umesh right, the sleeves riding and bunching around his biceps.

The thug to my right was a red-haired woman named Drew, another loyal employee of Regis Denayer. In contrast to Umesh, Drew wore blue-and-white street wear, tennis shoes ... and a scar that hadn't been there four years ago. It curved like a second smile across her left cheek.

Still squirming, I spewed out as many local cusswords as I could remember before a voice from one corner of the room froze those words on my tongue. And my blood in my veins.

"Little Shell. We've missed you so much."

Scuttle!

He'd been leaning a shoulder against the wall where the far right-hand end of Craig's bookshelves cast thick shadow. Now he came a few steps toward me. He wore that same expensive suit I'd seen yesterday. But he'd abandoned the slick-hair look, letting his shoulder-length curls fall to his shirt collar. His dead, gray eyes looked me over as his tongue flickered out to wet his lips. That tongue, I'd always thought, should have been forked.

I shifted attention to Craig. "You said he left ..."

And then it dawned. Like it should have yesterday. Craig was working with these maniacs—he was in their pocket. He was in *Daddy's* pocket. Scuttle might've left the previous afternoon, but that had been after Craig confirmed my presence here. And a ship like Scuttle's could have made it to Theseus and back in twenty-four hours easily. Dad had at least one HQ set up on Theseus. Which meant—

"Extra manpower," Scuttle confirmed, watching me put it together. "That's what I went for."

"Person power," Drew grumbled, her scarred cheek twitching with irritation.

"Shut up," he told her absently, without taking his eyes off me. They shifted toward my bare scalp. "Not sure I like the new look, Shelby."

"I do," Umesh said.

"Shut up," Scuttle repeated.

Craig cleared his throat. "I'd like to go now. I don't really need to be here for this."

Scuttle jerked his head toward the door. "It's your station. Do what you like." Umesh and Drew dragged me out of Craig's path as he gathered his heavy slab under one arm and made his exit. His stride was jerky, his cheeks flushed. He didn't glance my way.

After he'd gone, Scuttle gestured for his goons to release me. Drew gave me a shove toward Scuttle, forcing me to do a little dance to avoid him.

"Four years, Little Shell," Scuttle said, moving to one of Craig's armchairs and sinking into it. He crossed his legs. "Four years we've been looking for you. This means a big bonus for the three of us."

Umesh gave a low giggle at that, the noise perfectly suited to an imbecile.

Drew said, "A bonus I plan to spend on a holiday. I've done nothing *but* look for you this whole time, princess."

"That's true," Scuttle said. "You've kept her very busy. Some clever identity changes, by the way."

"Perhaps I can help you all," I said, crossing my arms. "Whatever Dad's offering, I'll up it. Double it? Then you can all take that holiday now. No waiting."

It was a bluff and a stupid one and—judging by the amusement in their eyes—they knew it as well as I did. Besides, no way were they going to cross Daddy for a few dollars more.

Scuttle said, "Funny you should mention extra money. We've got a few things to do here before we reunite you with your father." He said to the others, "Umesh, go help your brother upstairs. Drew, may I have a moment alone with Ms Denayer?"

"All the way outside?" Drew asked.

"Yup."

"But that carpet out there—"

"So, close your eyes. Dream of a Caultan ski slope."

She snorted and followed Umesh out. Once they'd locked the outer door behind them, Scuttle leered at me, looking me up and down. Not for the first time, I wondered what guys saw to leer at when I was dressed in work gear. He rose from the chair and approached me. I backed away until I was pressed against the wall.

He said, "Shelby Denayer. Going around calling herself Jackie Griffin. As if she's embarrassed by her real name. Her heritage."

"It's called creating a new life. That's what you do when you're on the run from sewage-scum like you." I flinched, wondering if he'd slap me: that at least it would give me some satisfaction, because the bruise he left might cost him a finger or two when Daddy saw it.

Scuttle gave no sign of hearing me. He carried on with his monologue as if he'd been rehearsing it for years and refused to have his performance interrupted. "I always cared for you Shel. You know I did. And I get why you left. I do. If *my* father had been marrying me off to a mudpig like Jefferson Dourani, I'd have run too. I'm just hurt that you didn't trust *me* to get you away safely." He came nearer, leaning in so close I could feel his soupy breath on my forehead, my eyes. "The offer I made back then still stands. Regis knows you're here, of course. But I can still get you away, if you say the word. Think about it. I can make you so safe he'll never find you again. Just you and me. If I can find you, I know how to hide you."

"Yeah," I croaked, my mouth dry. "You'd hide me. You'd hide me in a box. In a basement. No, thank you."

The slur diluted the smugness on his face. He stepped away. "Your father hasn't forgotten his plans for you. It's been a major embarrassment for him, being unable to honor the deal with the Dourani Family." He turned and his face had set hard as stone. "A week of marriage to that slime Jefferson and you'll be begging me to put you in a box in the basement." He sniffed. "The offer stands. But don't think about it too long. Daddy's gonna want to see you soon. He missed you too, sweet Shel, just like I did." He moved to Craig's inner door. "Meantime, I have work to do. It's a lucrative place, this. Lots of stuff not nailed down and asking to be taken. The Sol-system black market is always hungry for resources like they have here." From beside the lily, he waved me into the outer office. After I'd complied, he used a keycard to lock Craig's room. "Don't think Craig wants you sitting alone in there. And we have to keep him onside for the moment."

I'd heard the outer door lock behind Drew. If I ran from Scuttle, it would be straight into her. Slumping, I dropped into the assistant's chair. "The Prisoner of Zenda," I muttered.

"What?"

"You wouldn't understand."

"Probably a book reference. You do love those damn things. Anyways, Umesh is a bit busy right now, but he'll be down soon to take you to my ship."

Sure, I thought. *When the afternoon shift ends and the warehouse and hangars are even quieter.*

"Take it easy till he gets here," Scuttle continued. "Put your feet up. Contemplate your impending future as Jefferson Dourani's bride. And give my offer some serious thought. If you have anything to ask me, you can comm me privately from the Hellfish. I'll word Umesh up on that. Trust me, sweetheart, you call me, I'll answer. Now: I'll lock this outer door again. Don't try to pick it and run." He chuckled. "There's not really anywhere to run *to* out here. Is there?"

SIX

They'd removed the assistant's commset, cables and all. Probably before I even came in. However, it took me less than ten minutes to hack the workstation and access the intranet.

"Shouldn't have left me alone, scab suckers."

My chirpiness faded fast. Nothing I tried worked. I wrote a post for the station's Social Forum; the AI moderating the forum flagged it as a prank and issued me a 24-hour ban from social media. I contacted Security; no one answered either my call or my messages. That gave me a good idea about where Umesh and his brother Farouq were. And what they were doing.

I commed Toby. But Toby rejected my call.

I tried three other workmates. One rejected it, as Toby had. One didn't answer, probably because he was asleep. And the one who did pick up simply told me I should have checked the refit to Moretti's scarab, so it was me who'd killed him—then blocked me from calling back.

Next, I tried the Medical Centre up on Top Slice, but no one picked up. And I was partway through typing a message to them when the computer went blue-screen on me. There came an immediate tapping at the window. I looked up to see Drew wagging a finger in a *naughty naughty* gesture. She jerked a thumb behind her and moved from the window. I went to see what she'd pointed at: an open cabinet in the thoroughfare wall. Inside were fiber optic cables and some kind of device clamped on top of one of them. A jammer?

She wouldn't see me clearly through the window tinting, but she could no doubt see the blinds moving. She shot me a wink, then closed the cabinet flush with the wall before sinking onto her haunches. While I muttered imprecations, Drew pulled out a slim from the side pocket of her pants and started playing a game. I was halfway through another swear word when the sight of her slim reminded me that I had *my* slim in *my* work pants' side pocket.

"Hallelujah," I whispered and withdrew from the window.

The full wifi bars told me that Drew's jammer wasn't affecting my device. Daddy's thugs hadn't gotten smarter in the years since I'd seen them: none of them had bothered searching me for anything I might be carrying that was a threat to them. They still thought of me as Little Shell Denayer, the kid, the nobody, the weakling.

"Weakling *this*, buttholes," I said as I flicked on the messaging app Watson and I shared.

I tapped the URGENT icon and typed, *I'm in trouble. Bad. Need your help.*

Although he was sure to be asleep, or engrossed in a simulation, or in a mood, he *would* hear the loud URGENT chime. I expected him to respond quickly. He'd been there for me after Moretti died. We had always been there for each other in moments of crisis or despair.

No answer came. Not in the first minute. Not in the fifth. By the time the tenth minute was over, I knew he wasn't going to check the message. Was he so angry that he'd frozen me out completely? Could he be out at the Concourse? Or out working overtime? Last I'd seen him, he'd been storming out of our digs with his work knapsack over his shoulder. But he'd packed his slim; I'd seen him do it.

Panic setting in, I sank into a corner of the office, hugging my knees and making small moaning sounds. There wasn't anyone else I could contact who would take this seriously, the result of my reclusiveness. Even my hacking skills wouldn't connect my slim with the FTL transmitter up in the Olive. This was the end. The end of my little jaunt, my beautiful freedom. Four years I'd had and now my time was up. Foolish to think I could thwart my father forever. Foolish to think my life was my own.

I pinched my thigh and I punched it. It was disgusting, this display of self-pity, this sniveling weakness. I launched myself to my feet. The *doing-something* birthed an idea. Rifling through desk drawers, I found an aerosol can.

Sure, I thought with a nod. *That'll sting.*

I hate violence. I've always hated it. But sometimes a girl's gotta do what she's gotta do. If my only option was tricking Drew in here and blinding her with deodorant, then I was committed. Maybe I could still find Watson; we could figure out how to fly that Hellfish together.

Moving to the window, I had my hand raised to rap on it, and froze, surprised.

Drew was nowhere to be seen.

And Toby was sitting on the bench seat outside the chaplain's office.

SEVEN

Toby had his elbows on his thighs, his gaze on the orange carpet. What was he here for at this time of night? More counselling?

What did it matter why he was here? I activated the flashlight on my slim and angled it his way. It took him a moment but he saw it, frowning. I deactivated the light and got my face against the window, tapping with my slim.

A moment's hesitation when he saw a face squashed against the glass, a deepening of his frown, but he did rise, he did come over.

When he was close enough to recognize me, he snorted. "Griff? What the fleg?"

"Open the door. Please."

"What? Why? What are you doing in there?"

"Forget that, just open the door!"

He moved past me. The door rattled. "How?" he called through it.

I put my head against it and opened my mouth, expecting inspired words to emerge. None did. His question was a good one. Without a coded keycard, he wasn't getting in and I wasn't getting out. Unless …

A cutting laser. That'd work.

Before I had time to finesse a way of asking him to take a laser to the COO's office door, I heard another voice out there. My shoulders drooped. Drew was back.

There was friendly chitchat between them—I'd never noticed it before, but apparently Drew could turn on the charm when she needed to. I shifted to the window, trying to get his attention and signal him to run. But he wasn't looking.

I yelled, "Toby, run!"

He didn't seem to hear me.

Drew jerked her head at the door, a keycard in hand. She opened it. He was in mid-comment when she bundled him inside and locked us both in.

"What the—!"

"You idiot!" I cried and struck him in the chest.

Instantly, I felt a pang of remorse. *I* was the idiot. I'd just gotten him in more trouble than he'd ever been in.

A tap at the window. Drew reprised her *naughty naughty* gesture with a big grin on her face. Her scar seemed to glow a happy pink. I flipped her the bird before she withdrew to the bench that I'd dragged Toby from.

Beside me, Toby was incensed. "How am I an idiot? You called me over."

"Okay, okay, you're right."

He didn't seem to hear me, rattling the door. "And now I'm locked in here. What is this? What the hack have you gotten me into?"

"I—" My hands cupped my face as I gathered my thoughts. "Listen to me, Toby. We have to get away. Use your slim. Call someone. A friend. The med center. No one's listening to me."

His turn to shake his head and I knew what he'd say before he said it. "I left it at home. So I could do some thinking before I saw the Chaplain."

Growling in frustration, I tried Watson again on mine. Nothing. Holy crap, he'd never been this mad before.

"We have to get out of here," I told Toby. As if that wasn't already obvious.

He made a *How do we do that?* face.

A fresh idea came to me in the form of a memory, something Scuttle had done eight years before. The time he and Daddy and I had been stuck in the back of a bank at midnight when the guard returned early from a break. The guard had stood between us and escape as Drew did now.

The warehouse upstairs was a pretty cold place at all times. I'd donned a hoodie over my coveralls. Removing the sweater, I went behind the desk and fit it over the chair back, as if over a torso. "Turn down the lights," I told Toby.

"Why?"

"Do it!"

He turned the dial near him. The office darkened until I could barely make out his face.

Perfect.

I raised the height of the chair as far as it would go, then made the hood of my sweater stand up like a head, like someone was sitting there. I had the aerosol in hand, but I noticed then that the assistant had left their coffee mug on her desk. I picked it up. It was a heavy mug, dense, sturdy. Hitting Drew with this would be far more extreme than spraying deodorant in her eyes.

And much more effective.

I tossed the spray can aside.

Joining Toby again, I handed over my slim and pushed him to the window.

"Shine the flashlight at her eyes. Annoy the crap out of her. Try to dazzle her, so she's got bright spots in her vision."

He thumbed on the light. "Hope you know what you're doing."

"When she starts over here, sit on the desk with your hands up, but sit where she can see the ... fake person." I moved to the other side of the door as he began irritating Drew through the window. "The second the door opens, start complaining about the lights."

His only response was a long shuddering breath as he scurried over to the desk. He perched himself with arms folded.

I braced myself.

The door unlocked and slid into the wall. "Do you *want* me to kill you?" Drew started as she came inside.

"The lights aren't ..." Toby started.

Drew paused, frowning at the room's darkness. "What —?" I brought the mug down on the top of her head. One knee buckled, her right hand going to her head, but she stayed upright, reeling toward me. "You little—"

My next swing was low, roundhouse. The mug struck her in the ribs. As she curled over, trying to backpedal outside, I swung one last time at her head, catching her above an ear. She collapsed, moaning, down on hands and knees amongst the burnt orange shagpile.

"Griff!" Toby exclaimed, coming off the desk. Since Scuttle had started using my real name, *Griff* already sounded weird, foreign.

I booted Drew hard in the butt, tossing her on her face,

then removed a blackbeamer from its holster in the small of her back. The teardrop-shaped weapon fit snugly into my hand, cool and smooth to touch.

Still groggy, she rolled over. Blood streamed onto her face from the wound on top of her head. "Whaff? Whah doon? Bish!"

"Get up," I told her, examining her weapon further in the passageway light. I'd seen them before, but never held one. The shape, the weight, the feel, the power—it was seductive. The wretched things were exclusively for police or military use. Where did Dad get these? And how had Drew gotten one past the station's security systems?

Oh, right. Craig.

I waved it at her. "Get *up!*"

She did. In stages. Crawling to a wall. Getting an arm against it. Up on both knees. Up on one knee, then slowly finding her feet. All the while, I bobbed on the balls of *my* feet, wanting to scream at her, watching both ways along the corridor.

"There's an app on my slim," I told Toby. "EezySpeek. Mark the message URGENT and tell Watson to get his butt up to East Hangar *now*. Set it to alert him every five seconds till he turns off. Tell him ... Tell him, we're going for a ride in a Hellfish."

No arguments or questions from Toby this time. He typed as Drew found her balance. She was pretty conscious now—I knew this from the daggers she was glaring at me through the blood in her eyes.

"I'll use this, Drew." I waggled her gun. "I've got nothing to lose. And the universe won't miss you."

Her lip curled up from her teeth.

I gestured towards the lifts. She hobbled ahead of us, right arm extended toward the wall in case she stumbled.

Toby came up behind me. "Message sent."

"You set it to alert constantly? Annoy the hell out of him until he reads the damn thing?"

"Yes! No need to nag. Who are these people? What trouble are you in?"

"The trouble I'm in is the trouble *you're* in. We're heading out-system. Once we're safely somewhere else, you can give me a head start then report the whole thing to the cops."

"Out-system! I have a job! *Here!*"

"Your job will still be there once this is over. But you probably won't want to work for Craig. He's in bed with these people."

His mouth worked but no words came out. I could only imagine his shock. He'd come up here hoping to cry on the Chaplain's shoulder, only to get caught up in a crime family conflict.

At the elevators, I told him to punch the button then checked back the way we'd come. I wished I hadn't. Scuttle stood ten meters back. He too held a blackbeamer. But he was holding his at the Chaplain's head. Craig stood behind them, looking sheepish.

I bunched the material of Drew's shirt around my fist and spun her around, put the gun in her back.

"Where's that lift?" I asked Toby, not breaking eye contact with Scuttle. The scumbag was grinning. Oh, how I hated that grin.

"Um. Um. Thirty seconds away. Maybe."

A long time under the circumstances.

"Bad timing," Scuttle called out, "you leaving just as I'm

coming back. Also—" He pushed the barrel harder into Chaplain Montez's cheek, forcing a gasp. "—bad timing for this idiot, sticking his head out of his office as I'm sneaking up behind you."

"Maybe let the Chaplain go," I heard Craig say. Scuttle just snorted at the idea.

"Any closer?" I asked Toby.

He put his head to the door. "Can't hear it."

God, why did the elevators have to be so *slow* on this station?

Scuttle had an arm gripping Montez's elbow and he walked him closer.

"Stop there!" I called. This was really bad. I had never intended for anyone else to get caught in the perils of my father's search for me. I'd avoided close friendships, romantic attachments. Now Toby was caught up in it, and the poor Chaplain.

And—*oh God!*—what if Scuttle followed me to the hangar and Watson was up there. What if my little buddy got shot?

"Shelby, you know how this works." Scuttle came a tad closer. Craig followed behind, keeping Scuttle between himself and my weapon.

"Shelby?" Toby asked.

"My actual name."

"Crap. Who *are* you?"

"Let Drew go," said Scuttle, "and give her back the gun. Or this guy's head vaporizes."

"You wouldn't," I tried. "A weapon discharge sends an instant red flag to—"

"Security?" he finished. "You mean the guys that Umesh and Farouq have vented out a trash chute by now?"

"Dear Lord," the Chaplain gasped. "You murdered them?"

Scuttle roared with laughter. "I'm kidding, fella. Just kidding. They're all fine. Drugged and enjoying sweet, sweet dreams."

"Damn it," I hissed. Help really wasn't coming.

"Don't cave," Toby said, surprising me. "The lift's almost here. I can hear it."

"You get in that lift, Little Shell," Scuttle called, "and I kill this guy."

"*Damn it.*"

Toby touched my shoulder. "Griff, Shelby, whoever you are. Don't cave."

"Better cave," Drew said over her shoulder.

Scuttle's grin was fading as real anger surfaced in his expression. I heard the lift brake behind us. We were seconds away from relative safety. But I knew he'd do it. He would totally do it.

"Damn it!" I shouted.

I shoved Drew away. Bending, I placed the gun on the carpet where it sank halfway into the pile. Drew staggered across the passage to lean on the wall, either to get out of the firing line, or because she didn't trust herself to stay upright.

And Scuttle's grin was back in full force. He lowered the pistol from the Chaplain's face to the man's ribs, took his arm off the man's elbow. "See, that wasn't so hard, was it? Neither is this, by the way."

There came a dull *chut* sound, a flash of dark-light.

Something in my brain dislocated—as time slowed, as I stood aside from myself and watched the Chaplain's tunic puff out from his chest, a cloud of vaporized body tissue bursting from the new hole in that tunic.

"No!" I heard myself say. I think Toby said it too.

Montez staggered aside and away from Scuttle, staring down at the spreading dark patch on his tunic, his mouth hanging open. Another step away. Another. I think he was going for the wall, the same way Drew had. He didn't make it. On the next step, his legs betrayed him. He collapsed in a heap, eyes fixed on me. Yesterday he had looked at me with indignation; this time however, there was compassion in his eyes. Or perhaps something beyond that. Perhaps it was pity. Eventually, I realized his eyes were staring, just staring, nothing in them. The man was gone.

Also, the lift doors were closing. I hadn't noticed them open.

My awareness seemed to piece itself together. I turned, hoping Toby wouldn't be there, hoping he'd ducked inside the elevator while he'd had the chance.

But Toby's feet were rooted to the floor, his arms spread wide as if waiting for a hug, his eyes fixed on the Chaplain's body. Smoke ribboned upwards from the black hole in the side of his tunic. The hallway air stank of burned fat and scorched hair.

Scuttle ventured even closer, halfway between me and his victim. "You rat-bastard," I hissed.

He waggled his eyebrows. "No witnesses. You know how Regis operates."

Craig—who had been frozen to the spot like Toby—barked something between a laugh and a sob. His eyes tracked the cloud of body tissue settling toward the carpet. "No witnesses? No witnesses! You've left a huge bloody scorch mark on the wall there, this shit all over my carpet! And how are you going to get rid of the body?"

Scuttle kept coming toward me. Toby backed away and out of my peripheral vision. I stayed still.

"We don't need to," Scuttle said. "I have the beginnings of an idea." He started circling me, forcing me to turn my head to keep him in view. "I have a very good idea. For the time being, for as long as it's useful to us, Ms *Griffin* here is a suspect in the murder of ... what was his name?"

I said nothing.

Toby answered. "Chaplain Petruso Montez."

"Chaplain? Wow. Even better."

"You're crazy, Scuttle," I snarled.

He chuckled. "*You're* crazy, Ms Griffin. You killed the chaplain. Naughty naughty."

"Naughty, naughty," Drew growled from her place against the wall. She had a hand pressed to the top of her head. I now wished I'd hit her harder. I could have tried getting into her ship without her help.

I said, "How are you going to make that nonsense stick?"

Scuttle clicked his tongue. "Easily explained. See, you came to the Chaplain to confess that it was your *mistake* that killed that Moretti guy. Craig told me about him, by the way. When the Chaplain told you he had to report all criminal offences, even negligence, you went nuts. Shot him." He chuckled again, pointing to Montez's corpse. "Got rid of a witness."

"Where did she get the gun?" Toby asked, voice wavering. I half-turned his way. His jaw was set defiantly. He was a few meters behind me now. But he wasn't running. Maybe he rightly thought Scuttle would blast him if he did.

Scuttle squinted at him. "Who are you, exactly?"

Toby clammed up.

Drew said, "He was waiting outside the dead guy's office

before I could lock this area off. She got his attention by shining her flashlight at him." She winced and I wondered if it was because of a stab of pain, or because of embarrassment at me duping her with the same method.

"Oh," said Scuttle. "So, he's no one." He aimed at Toby's head.

"No!" I cried as Toby flinched and ducked.

Scuttle lowered the gun without firing. "Hm. Maybe not no one. I think Shelby has a friend. But what she sees in it, I don't know." To Drew, he added, "Head okay?"

"Gettin' there."

He scooped up her handgun and carried it across to her. "You still have that cop badge?"

She holstered the weapon and felt inside her thigh pocket before producing a United Nations Star Marshall wallet and badge.

"Good. For the moment, our ship is a Marshall vessel. Take these two up there and flash the badge if anyone intervenes."

"How long am I holding them for?" Drew's sneer said she didn't fancy any more babysitting.

"As long as I say."

"Can't Umesh do it? I'm due for a break here. Maybe see the doctors." She touched her head again.

He narrowed his eyes at her. "The brothers are busy up in the 'Olive' now. You don't remember that?"

She grunted. "Small concussion. I'll be fine." A moment later, she added, "What are they doing again?"

"They're wrecking the subspace transmitter. You *sure* you can handle Shelby this time?"

Drew's sneer was back. "I really hope she tries something."

"That's better," Scuttle said.

"What about ... you know. The blood?" She turned her palm to show him, as if he couldn't see the half-liter of it all over her head.

"Part of the show. Anyone asks, you show 'em the badge and tell 'em these two resisted arrest." He winked at me. "You're dangerous people, Ms Griffin. I'd hate to get on the wrong side of you."

EIGHT

Drew took us up the passenger lift, herding us into the corner while she covered us from beside the controls. This lift opened onto the packing area just outside the warehouse floor and directly below East Hangar. To get to the hangar bays, we'd have to change elevators.

As we stepped outside, I could see two other scrappers—Maguire and Ali—over by the closest conveyor belt and doing as little work as possible. The belt was moving but they weren't putting anything on it, hands in pockets, chit-chatting about something.

"You say anything to anyone, and it looks like they believe you," Drew said, "I'll shoot them. Want that on your conscience?"

My reply was to bare my teeth at her.

Toby answered, "We don't, ma'am."

"Ma'am?" Drew huffed a laugh and signaled us to get moving. "I like polite assholes. Manners might just keep you alive, kid."

I couldn't let her trap us on that ship of theirs. It wasn't just the fact that she and Scuttle were about to hand me over to Daddy again, or that Dad intended to marry me off to a bigger psychopath than he was. It was Toby. I'd dragged him into this. I had to get him out of it. Despite what she'd just told him, Drew would vent him out an airlock and forget what he looked like thirty seconds later. As we preceded her across the floor toward the smaller elevator on the far side, I scanned my environment for a way to hurt her again. I abhor violence, I do. The worst thing I ever did was slap one of Dad's goons for sassing me. Before today, before Scuttle had shot the Chaplain, I'd felt guilty just stepping on ants. Not now. Now was different. I could feel something uncoiling within me, a darkness maybe, a hardness, something I'd never known.

We were *not* going on that ship. No matter what it took to stay off it.

One option for ridding ourselves of Drew was the moving conveyors. Perhaps, I thought, I could knock her into the moving gears and plates beneath. I shuddered at that. Too gruesome. And very hard to pull off.

Before I could think of anything else, we were passing the first conveyor, drawing stares from Maguire and Ali, transfixed by Drew's matted hair and blood-streaked face.

"Mind your business," she snapped at them.

Maguire called her a name I won't repeat.

But Ali blinked as he recognized me. "Hey. Griffin. If you guys are looking for that chimp of yours, don't bother. He stole a garbage scow and vanished with it. He's in a world of trouble."

I stopped and gaped at him. Drew cursed me.

"They probably already know that, dumbass," Maguire piped up. He raised his voice and directed the next questions to Drew. "That how ya got messed up? That chimp hit ya?"

"Keep moving," she told Toby and me. We did.

My heart pounded even harder. A scow? The damn things were used to carry trash from the station and cast it toward the local star. What was Watson thinking? Did he think he could escape the system in it? Those things didn't have FTL drives.

Oh, honey, I thought. *Be safe.*

It was near the second conveyors that I saw my opportunity. Someone had left their forklift running at the end of the second belt, directly in our path. No sign of the driver, possibly on a bathroom break. Leaving a powered-up fork unattended was the kind of breach that would get you an official warning and fine during day shift. After ten o'clock at night, when Management were either at a restaurant or in bed, scrappers tried it on pretty regularly. Saved time running through all the close-down/start-up checklists.

Thank you, lazy bum, whoever you are.

"Drew," I said. "That's the fork I was using before Craig called me downstairs."

"Wow. That's so interesting." She pressed her hand to her head again, face screwed up.

"I just want to get my bag out of it. Please? It has my ... hygiene products." My glance at Toby was intended to feign embarrassment. But I winked with the eye Drew wouldn't see. He gulped and looked away.

"Whatever," she said. "But you run and lover boy here dies resisting arrest."

"As Scuttle said, where am I gonna go?"

"Just sayin'. I've had as much bullshit as I'm gonna take from you today."

Oh, no you haven't, I thought. *Not if I can help it.*

As we neared it, I mumbled out the side of my mouth, "Get ready to drop to the floor."

"Bloody hell," Toby moaned quietly.

"What was that?" asked Drew.

"Nothing, just apologizing for talking about sanitary products in front of him."

"Buddha help us," she muttered. "Hurry the hell up."

It was *going* to be hurried, I thought as I scrambled into the forklift's cab. And it was going to be close.

While my right hand fished for a non-existent bag beneath the driver's seat, my left activated the hologram controls beside the wheel. I made a series of gestures, pre-programming the sequence with haste and what I hoped was accuracy. Then my right hand gripped the seat hard and my left activated the sequence.

The forklift's wheels snapped right and the little vehicle made a quick dart that way, skipping sideways a meter closer to Toby and Drew. Both opened their mouths in surprise. For a split second, I thought Toby might react too late, or not at all. This model's tines were fitted to tracks that ran around the entire chassis. They whipped around to the right and Toby dropped beneath them. Drew did not. The rightmost tine—a eighty-kilogram length of hard steel—smashed into Drew as she raised her gun-arm. The tine slipped beneath that arm and crashed into her ribs, tossing her like a rag doll to land three meters away.

I hit the safety-stop and jumped out, dragging Toby from the floor. "All right?"

"Oh, God," he replied. "Better than her."

Drew was curled up on one side, making ghastly staccato noises. A pink froth oozed from her mouth, which opened and closed like that of a landed fish. Her personal slim poked from one of her trouser pockets; on a whim I grabbed it, then scanned the area for the gun. It lay a few meters further out, back toward the first conveyor. I scurried over, picked it up—and looked straight up into Ali's eyes. He too had bent to retrieve something. Drew's Star Marshall badge which had skipped further along the floor.

"Griff?" he said. "Griff, what the fleg!"

"It's not ... She's not ..." I was backing away. The gun was out in front of me, pointed his way. What the hell was I doing? I couldn't stop aiming it. And I couldn't stop backing away. Beyond Ali, I saw Maguire running for the alarm button back by the passenger lifts. We had to get to the hangar and into the Hellfish.

I fled, snaring Toby's arm as I passed and dragging him with me. "Hangar lift," I snapped.

"Oh, God," he repeated.

Behind me came shouts. "Stop her! Stop them! They killed a Star Marshall!"

The closest bathrooms were beside the goods elevators; a woman I knew emerged. Her name wouldn't come to me. Probably the fork driver. For some reason, as we locked eyes I said, "Sorry!"

Seeing the gun, she ran hard in another direction.

The lift was at our level, opening the moment I slapped the button. No one inside. We darted in and smacked more buttons, me the *hangar level* button, Toby the *close doors*.

As it rose, we panted and leaned our hands on our thighs.

"What are we doing?" Toby wheezed.

"Surviving," I wheezed back.

The doors opened again and we bolted out, swinging

right when we saw the sleek Hellfish parked in the rear, away from the bulkier craft. A half dozen people were working up here. Heads turned.

At the Hellfish's hull, Toby searched along the landing struts for a control for the access ramp while I tried hacking Drew's slim in case it was connected to the sleek cruiser. Neither of us had any luck. A warehouse alarm had started up. Although no one would know immediately what it was for, workers were already checking slims for advice.

"We're not gonna make it inside," Toby said.

"You're right," I groaned. Any minute now, an announcement would come through the intranet feeds or a speaker. Workers would obstruct us, or at least report us. Scuttle would come looking.

"There!" I barked, grabbing Toby's hand, pulling him along with me. A blue-clad tech stepped into the alley between ships we were taking. I was forced to let go of Toby's hand as we broke formation to sprint either side of the startled man.

"We're taking this!" I said, sprinting harder along and under the Bigmouth closest to the blue haze of the hangar exit's magnetic shield. I clomped up the access ramp. When Toby made it up onto the arterial deck with me, I told him to fire up the engines while I sealed us in. As the ramp curled up into the hull, I glanced at the serial number stenciled into the control panel. WK147B. This wasn't just any Bigmouth. WK147B was our Bigmouth, the one Moretti should have returned to the other day after a routine work shift.

I wondered, was that good omen or bad?

A tremor ran through the ship as Toby ignited the maneuvering engines.

NINE

WE WERE DRIFTING.

Earlier, we'd pushed the Bigmouth hard for ten minutes toward Mining Cluster 27 where Moretti had died. We'd then made the dangerous but necessary decision to turn off our responder, our *trans*ponder, our AI-assist, and all of our running lights. That allowed us to change direction without anyone knowing: to save system resources, the station's sensors marked local craft with a tag-and-forget marker, focusing instead on stray pieces of space junk, rogue rock chunks, debris, unknown ships.

Toby had turned us to starboard and slightly "north" from the system's orbital plane. It took both of us to fly her for the next hour, steering around warning buoys and across a network of flight lanes, squeezing between flight lane markers, relying on instruments alone while nervous sweat dampened our shirts and we traded data updates constantly.

After that hour, we were finally well away from collision hazards. The way ahead was clear; any stray object coming across our path would be picked up by sensors with time for us to avoid it. We could afford to cut engines and coast.

And so, we drifted at the speed we'd built up to. Slumped in our chairs, silent, wrung out. I noticed Drew's gun, wedged in the meeting point of control console and canopy housing. When had I put it there? Was that a good place for a gun? Had I really hit her with a forklift? I felt the dull impact between tines and flesh transmitted through the vehicle's frame. I heard the sound, the *oof* of air from her lungs and the muffled thud and scrape of her hitting the floor and rolling. I saw the pink froth upon her lips. And I stamped down hard on that that crap, stamped it down deep within me, snatching up the gun, sliding out of my seat and around the ladderwell and stuffing the weapon into one of the shallow cupboard-compartments along the bulkhead.

As I leaned there, breathing hard, with broken thoughts swirling around my mind, Toby chose that moment to ask his question. The only question, I'm sure, that mattered to him there and then.

"Why?"

I passed a palm across my bald scalp. Once. Twice. Thrice. Returned to my chair. "Why run? Or why is this happening?"

"Both!"

One more rub of the head, then I clasped my hands together, wringing them. "We're running because they're framing us for murder. With what I did to Drew, probably two murders. What else can we do but keep our distance until the authorities arrive in-system and we can clear our names?"

"*Our* names?"

"You were with me when … when I killed Drew."

He slouched deeper. "Clear our names," he whispered.

"Yeah."

I hoped that was something we could do. Or else, the greatest irony of my life would be that my father never went to jail but I did.

"And?" he said. He was leaning away from me, nostrils flaring. One eye ticced. "What's the reason those freaks are after you?"

I blew out a breath. Took another. Blew that out too. "There's something about me you don't know."

"Obviously."

I hadn't buckled my harness. It hung from the side of my chair, as limp as my spirit. I wound a hand through it, twisting it around my fingers. "If you'd known what I'm about to tell you, no way would you have hit on me, Toby. Not in a million years."

"I never 'hit on you'! I asked you out!"

Maybe he didn't remember that drunken visit to my door. Releasing the harness, I made a *calm-down* motion. "It doesn't matter. Either way, I'm not the kind of girl you brag about to your parents."

He waited me out, breath whistling in and out of his nostrils. His pupils were large and that eye kept on ticcing.

"I'll bullet point the main concepts," I told him. "Less you know the better. My father is a very bad man. A gangster. Those three were his ... employees. Dad—" I almost said *Daddy*, but bit back on the second syllable. "—had plans to marry me off to an even worse man. Kind of like when ancient kings married off their daughters to seal pacts with other countries."

I paused for breath as Toby's eyes softened. He whispered, "Holy crap."

"So, I bolted the first chance I got, when I was twenty years old. Four years, that's how long I've been out. I'd started thinking I might be safe. Finally. But obviously my father's people never stopped looking for me."

He rubbed at the eye with the tic and turned his head toward the canopy, his gaze toward the void. "So, we have to stay out here until the cops come."

"And hope there's enough evidence back there to prove it was those animals who killed the Chaplain, not us."

He gave a little whimper at that.

Hastily, I added, "There will be. I'm sure there will be. Definitely."

We lapsed into silence. Like many people abruptly thrust into catastrophe, my mind started on a litany of *if onlys* ...

If only I'd left yesterday. I'd had a chance. I'd had a warning. I'd had a head start. *But how could I possibly have left without a scheduled transport?* I asked myself. The answer was I could have stolen one of the large FTL freighters parked outside The Sandwich. *Now you think of that?* I scolded. Well, it was a dumb idea anyway. I could fly a relatively simple Bigmouth, but what did I know about freighters? And FTL travel, leaping out of the star system? I'd have smeared the ship and me across a light-minute of space. Also, the freighters had crews.

Thinking of ship-theft led me to my next *If Only*. If only I'd gotten access to Scuttle's ship. I couldn't fly it. But, we might have barricaded ourselves in and used the FTL transmitter to contact the Corporate Union's police force or the Star Marshalls. But I hadn't done that. I'd done what I'd always done. Since first slipping away from Daddy on that vacation to Foucault's Moon. I'd run. My constant and only plan was to run and work out the rest later—and what a crappy plan it was.

I sighed quietly, so Toby wouldn't notice.

He'd gotten his question out of the way. Now that I had time to think, I had questions of my own. Two of them.

Where was Watson?

And would the little guy eventually return to the station where Scuttle could hurt him?

Please be okay, I thought toward him. *Please sneak aboard a freighter or something. Stow away until it heads out-system. Like I should have got us to do yesterday.*

Could Toby and I still do that? No way. Besides the fact it would mean abandoning Watson, hiding on a freighter would only corner us. At least out here in the void, we could keep moving with a *lot* of space to do it in.

"So, we'll wait out here for the cops to come," I said.

Toby grunted. He'd turned away from me, fingers tapping his forehead.

My heart already felt like it had dropped into my stomach but it sank further at a new thought. Whether or not the cops came to my rescue this time, they would keep tabs on me afterwards; they wouldn't let me disappear even if Daddy did. And if *they* knew where I was, Daddy only had to buy one of them off to find me again. Craig had demonstrated that anyone could be bought.

Staring into the black emptiness of space, I asked myself, *Where in the cosmos do we go now?*

As if he'd read my mind, Toby answered me. "I know a place."

TEN

THE FREE-FLOATING asteroid Toby told me about didn't appear on any company maps. So I was skeptical about its existence. And suspicious for the first few minutes after he'd punched in the coordinates. Craig had been bought. How did I know that Toby hadn't been also?

But that was a dumb thought. He had been genuinely horrified over the Chaplain's death. He'd helped me against Drew. And he was still plainly terrified: as he double-checked the coordinates he'd entered, his face was three shades paler than usual, his eyes wide in dismay. Also, he'd turned the transponder off so we couldn't be tracked.

No. Toby was in as much crap as I was. He wasn't a mole.

Then how did they find you? whispered a little voice in the back of my head. I had no answer for it. So, I let the possibility remain a possibility, even as I went along with his course change. I mean, I didn't have any better ideas.

It took five long hours to reach the rock. For most of those five long hours, we alternated between three activities: pacing the main passage, fixing each other hot beverages, and sitting slumped in our chairs gazing literally into nothing. Then finally, shipnav noticed the 'roid right where Toby said it would be, announcing it with a small melody and a text announcement across our screens. Fifteen minutes later, I saw a speck of gray against the black. Sixteen minutes later, I could make out a white warning light blinking on one end of it. Eighteen minutes and I could tell the light was actually a group of lights.

I bent over the data feeds as we slowed to approach. "This thing's fifty light-seconds from the closest worksites. Almost fifteen million km. And moving away from them. It's an orphan."

Toby just grunted.

The rock grew large in our viewports and the Bigmouth angled toward a circle of work lights that lay dead center of its mass—center from our perspective, that is. A cliché for describing asteroids is that they are potato-shaped. But this one wasn't: from our angle, it looked more like one of those bath ducks kids play with. It had a tail, and a head with a bill and everything.

"If you tell me you call this thing The Duck, I'll kill you."

He made a face. "Kill me then."

"It's an orphan. So how do you know about it?"

"I was out here. Last month."

"What the hell were you doing way out here?"

"Survey and prep-fitting. Sometimes I pull extra shifts to come and mark individuals like this or help install airlocks and access tunnels."

"What? You never told me you do that."

It was hot in the cockpit. He wrapped his arms about himself as if he were cold. "Don't tell you everything. Not like we're friends or anything."

That stung. More than I would have expected it to. I opened my mouth to object, but held my tongue, considering it.

Were we friends? What *was* a friend in Shelby Denayer's world?

Sure, we'd played futsal together, played cards, gone to a couple of Craig Parties together to laugh at the COO's poor athletic ability. Pleasant company, that's what we'd shared. Before the awkwardness after he'd asked me out.

Before my true identity had put his life in danger.

Okay. We weren't friends. I could accept that.

Watson had been my friend and he was gone.

Toby now resented and maybe hated me—with good reason.

Friends were not a concession the universe granted Shelby Denayer. I had always thought of close attachments as a threat to my safety. And now it was occurring to me that I was the threat to theirs.

I put some gentle interest into my voice. "You came out here by yourself?"

At my tone, his defensiveness ratcheted down a couple of notches, his arms unwinding. "For survey, yeah. I like it that way. Time alone. Time to ... think."

"But that's dangerous, guy."

He shrugged. "Survey craft only hold one person. Management thinks if an accident kills everyone on one, they're better off making 'everyone' one person. Why risk two lives?"

I was surprised they didn't use teams of chimpanzats. Or otteroons. Overseen by an AI.

"Two lives," I snorted softly. "Two lawsuits you mean."

He acknowledged that with the ghost of a grin. "Yeah, that too."

The shared moment of cynicism warmed me up a little, took the edge off the loneliness for a few precious moments.

Toby handed control over to me and raised one arm to point at something. "See the part there? The Duck's tail? The beacon light on the tip? If you vector around and lock orbit with that, you'll see an opening big enough for a scarab to enter and land. Another crew fitted an airlock in there, then I helped create a sealed survey tunnel. We go in there, we can exit into atmosphere. It'll be a bit cold, but survivable. The tunnel's only about fifty meters long, but it has lighting and it's pressurized."

"You're saying the entry's under The Duck's tail?"

"So?"

"You want us to take a scarab up a duck's butt?"

He grimaced. "You didn't have to put it like that."

"I've had the crappiest day ever, so yeah, I did have to put it like that."

I brought the Bigmouth around like he told me too, matching velocity and roll to that of the slowly spinning giant boulder. We donned e-suits as a precaution, then squeezed into a scarab.

Because he'd been here before, Toby piloted the little collector. I stooped behind him, gripping the chair to anchor myself in zero G. The beacon flashed from the tip of the outcrop Toby had called a tail. He pulled in beneath it. The beacon looked tiny from a long way out, but up close its housing was twice the size of our runabout. Now that Toby had named this area The Duck's tail, I couldn't unsee it—any more than I could unthink the idea we were flying into an enormous colon. The opening looming ahead was large enough to admit three scarabs side-by-side, ringed by smaller marker lights and open to the vacuum.

Toby's approach and landing were flawless, smooth. Within the roughly hewn hangar, he swung our vehicle's backend around to link with the airlock. Mating connectors did their thing; landing grapples snaked from the small craft's edges to hook us onto anchor-lugs bolted into the rock walls. Toby powered down engines, left the craft on standby and followed me to the rear hatch, which I cranked open. We wore our helmets, not wanting a disastrous day to turn catastrophic.

The airlock was bright with tiny lights, but when the inner hatch hissed open, I discovered that the tunnel beyond was not lit at all. Beyond the spillover illumination from within the airlock, the shaft curved out of sight and into darkness. I looked askance at Toby.

He said, "There's construction lights at the far end."

He tapped controls on his arm, firing up the suit's chest-lamp. Aiming the beam onto a wall-mounted VAC (Ventilation, and Air Conditioning) panel, he turned that on too. Then he headed for the tunnel bend without further comment. After triggering my own chest-lamp, I followed.

The passage floor was flat and four meters wide, its roof and walls curved in an arch. All surfaces had been coated with insulate-foam and the floor was laid with arti-grav mats. A yellow equipment case lay flipped open against the right-hand wall just before the bend. It was empty. Near it, my boot came down on a discarded rivet the size of my index finger—a half-meter slice of red-coated wiring lay near it. Some worker had burned the initials *BBB* with a laser into the insulation above me. A little further on, more initials. *DD*. Could have been anyone, since there were at least five hundred scrappers employed by The Sandwich at any given time. Then again, the initials may have been surveying markings for all I knew.

When I reached it, the passage bend proved to be a gentle one, and the shaft straightened out beyond it. Why, I couldn't tell. Why not cut a straight line? What *was* obvious, even with my limited knowledge of survey, was that this was a "staging chamber", laid quickly in preparation for future mining of The Duck.

Toby paused halfway along the second stretch of tunnel, facing a control panel bolted to the wall. Cables trailed from it into the open area at the tunnel terminus. One of Toby's hands rested on the board, but he hadn't switched on any lights. His faceplate was turned my way.

What's up with him? I wondered.

And then I drew level and my chest-lamp's beam revealed what lay at the tiny cavern's far end. A blanket, spread flat. A small space heater, not yet powered up. Two beanbags. A picnic basket. Four big candles, unlit.

"What's all this?" I asked.

He jolted as if stung and flipped two switches. The construction lamps flared to life and he turned off his chest-lamp. Unlocking and removing his helmet, he tested the air before finally answering my question. "Supplies. We won't starve here."

"Supplies? There's consumables on the Bigmouth." I slapped my faceplate in a moment of irritation, the thought occurring to me that we could have stayed on the ship and hidden the damn thing *behind* The Duck. No one could spy it then, not without coming out here.

I hadn't been thinking straight. The adrenaline, the shock, the high emotions of the past three days—the idea of running to something and hiding inside it must have scratched some kind of survival-instinct itch. But now, the adrenaline was ebbing, my heart was slowing, and I was starting to think clearly again.

Thinking clearly, all right: a new realization dawned. The blanket, the beanbags, the heater and picnic basket ...

Without noticing I'd walked to it, I stooped over the basket. Lifting the lid confirmed my sudden suspicion. Inside were freeze-dried foods, enamel coffee mugs, and a bottle of red wine and two glasses. I swung toward Toby, putting a hand over my chest-lamp's beam when he raised an arm to ward it off. "This is where you wanted to take me. When you asked me out. You had this all set up, waiting for me—"

Stunned by the wounded expression on his face, I bit off the flow of words. I switched off my lamp but he still didn't meet my eyes through my visor. Though he blinked away spots, I was sure he could see me just fine in the work lights' glow. He'd left his helmet by the lighting panel. His gloved hands fluttered at his side as if needing something to occupy them. And yes, where his cheeks had been pale with shock not so long ago, they were now flushed with embarrassment. He hadn't just asked me out casually; this had *mattered* to him.

You big twit. You big, dumb twit.

I cleared my throat and turned away, changing the subject. "Yep. Supplies. That's excellent. Good job, Tobester."

"I thought we might be out here a while—"

"Could be, yes."

"—and being in here might feel safer than sitting out there in the Bigmouth."

"I get that. Like a nest. A cave."

"Exactly."

"Human survival instinct for millions of years, sheltering in caves."

"Right."

"Excellent thinking."

I fell silent, as awkward as he. Needing to keep my hands busy also, I detached my helmet, took a long time positioning it by a wall, dusted it off.

"Um," he said, "you wanna sit?"

"Sure." I lowered myself into a beanbag. Not bad. Pretty comfy. Even while swaddled in an e-suit.

He dragged his a half-meter away before sitting in it.

On the way over, I had tried a couple of times to hack Drew's slim. But my heart hadn't been in it—I'd been too distracted, too exhausted. Now, I needed something to do. I pulled it from one of the suit's work-pouches. While Toby lapsed into unknowable thoughts, I tried every trick I knew. One worked—after forty minutes of screwing around, the home screen appeared.

"Aha!" I cried, triumphant. "Let's look at her emails."

A quick flip through them showed me a penchant for gambling (no surprise) and a new love affair with Umesh's brother, Farooq (a surprise). There was one at the top from Regis Denayer, my wonderful (gag!) father, and I avoided it at first. When I finally opened and read it, I groaned. The message was a group one, to Drew, to the brothers, to Scuttle. In barely coded language, Daddy Dearest agreed with Scuttle's assessment that Bissouma-Douglas had outsmarted themselves, that in laying claim to a far-flung star system's resources and putting a station here, they had opened themselves up to robbery on a grand scale. In fact, he was astonished (*lung-vacuumed*, was his term for it) that no other hold-up gangs had found their way here yet.

"He always did like to be the first to think of something," I mumbled.

"What?" Toby asked.

I dropped the slim on the lap of my suit and stretched, making the beanbag *shoosh* and morph. "Just reading Drew's messages."

"Oh yeah?"

"Seems my father's not content with just retrieving me. Now that Scuttle's worked his way in with Craig and had a good look at the inventory, Dad wants to steal as much as he can." I frowned at that. How much did ol' Regis expect Scuttle to carry off in a little craft like his? Our station had a decent inventory full of metals including nickel, manganese, cobalt, gold, platinum and rhodium. But they were in very large packages.

I scooped up the slim and scrolled to the bottom of the message. The next groan was louder and longer.

"Dad is coming," I told Toby. "And he's bringing his whole crew with him!"

ELEVEN

"WELL, WE'RE WAY OUT HERE," Toby replied. "Middle of nowhere and up a duck's ass—your words."

"Think I said 'butt'."

"Whatever. So, we're safe. There can't be enough of his guys to scour the entire system."

"That's not the problem. *We're* not the problem." I rubbed at my scalp, then stopped instantly when the rock dust I had on my gloves left scratches. I patted the skin with my sleeve, checked it. No blood, thank God. "Dad won't leave witnesses to this grand theft. That's one reason he's gotten away with so much bad crap for so long. He'll kill everyone on The Sandwich. From the last figures I saw, that's six hundred and twenty-five people!"

"Six hundred and twenty," Toby muttered.

"What?"

His beanbag hissed beneath him as he stirred. "Well, you and I aren't there. And Craig's working for them. And, you know, Moretti ... he isn't there anymore. Or the Chaplain."

"Shut up," I said, my gloved hands fluttering before me now like huge moths. "Shut *up*. Stop doing math. This is no time for math."

"Okay, okay. Stay on topic, I get it. But your Dad would need maybe a hundred goons to take control of The Sandwich and rob it. Sorry: math again. Just saying, he can't have that many people in his operation."

"He had a lot more than that, last time I knew. But actual thugs he can call on? Maybe sixty. I think he could do it with sixty. Hell, knowing my father, he could do it with forty. Now I think about it, all he needs to do is four things." I began ticking them off on my fingers. "First, pay off some inside men to help him. Second, cut off communications with the rest of the Union—"

Toby groaned: Scuttle had seen to both those things.

"Third, take control of key points around the facility to stop people getting in or out, or messing with climate control or whatever. Or getting messages out. That includes the two freighters holding off the East Hangar."

"Minimal bridge crews on freighters. That Scuttle guy could probably take them all on by himself." Toby had his gloves to his head now. "He could jam their comms, too."

I nodded. "And four, make sure his guys are the ones with all the guns. With Security taken out, that's not hard. Then they herd the facility's staff into central locations where they can easily watch them. Or kill them. And once he's got control and he's got all the guns, it's not hard to make a dozen scrappers do the heavy lifting. Literally. He can make them load up the smaller Bissouma-Douglas transports in West Hangar. Or one of those big freighters. Or he might bring his own cargo ship. If they do it right, they could leave with three full ships inside of one shift." It was a tad scary how easily the strategies came to me, how ready my brain was to conjure them.

"How in hell would they sell all that loot?" Toby asked. "He'd have thousands of tonnes of it."

"Dad's been at this a long time."

"But ... if they do all that ... they'll have their asses sticking out. What if an actual Marshall ship turns up in the middle of it?"

"When was the last time one of them appeared out here?"

He deflated a little, knowing the answer was *never*. Persisting, he asked, "What about a company bighead? Or a U.N. health-and-safety inspector? Or a new freighter?"

I was shaking my head. "If bigheads and safety inspectors turn up, they get lured in by one of Dad's goons in the comms center, then they're captured like everyone else. New freighter? There isn't one due for three days—I checked the schedules—and even if one did, they run mainly on automation as you said, with small crews."

He nodded unhappily. "So, it's not too hard for him to board them and take their crew captive as well. Crap."

A beanbag was a great place to sag. I sagged. Gravity felt more real this low to the floor, pulling me down. While standing, I'd experienced a little vertigo—when you work in space, you either get used to vertigo or you go home—but down here in a beanbag against the arti-grav mats, I felt stuck, I felt heavy. The feeling mixed well with my burgeoning despair.

"We haven't really gotten away," I said.

"*We* are the lucky ones," he said. "We're safe here."

I wasn't buying it. Even if we managed to elude Dad, the authorities would hold us at least partly responsible. They'd be looking for scapegoats, and my relationship to Regis Denayer made me an easy target. And if I escaped that somehow, if I tried to move on, Daddy would be out there, waiting for me.

"What the hell am I going to do?" I murmured into my palm. It was rhetorical, an expression of my wretchedness, but Toby responded anyway.

"Gotta be something. You'll think of something. I mean whoever your father is, you got away from him in the first place. That can't have been easy."

Oh, it wasn't, I thought. Eight months of planning. Paying off three minor officials. Arranging false IDs from a guy who hated Dad. Stowing away in a cattle-carrier off planet. It had taken ingenuity, planning, and courage.

And it was all for nothing!

I told him, "There's nada we can do. Zip. We can't fight the force that is my father."

What I really meant was, *I can't fight the force that is my father.*

The wine in the basket caught my eye. I yanked it free and uncorked it, drank straight from the bottle. It was dry and hard and as I gulped it down, it warmed my chest and my neck. I only stopped drinking when I needed to breathe, placing the bottle beside my legs, welcoming the buzz already starting.

Toby glared at me.

"What's the problem?" I snapped. "I'm disrespecting your precious wine? Not drinking it right?"

"I don't care about the damn wine," he snapped back. He pointed at the tunnel wall, *through* the tunnel wall. "I care about the fact that your dad and his gorillas are going to kill hundreds of people back there."

Yeah, I thought. *I'm none too thrilled about that either.*

"And we're just sitting here hiding," he continued.

The Duck had been his idea, but I wasn't going to hit him with that fact. I said, "Toby—"

"We're just gonna sit here and do nothing even though we know what's coming."

"*Toby!*"

I barked it, a lot harder than I intended. He clamped his jaw shut, but still glared at me. As if this were my fault.

It isn't, I told myself. *I'm not responsible for my father's evilness. Or what he does.*

But ...

"I'm responsible for what I know," I whispered, putting my head in my gloved hands.

Six hundred people out there, cut off from the galaxy, unaware of the storm that was coming. *Six hundred* people.

And one chimpanzat.

I was twenty-four years old. Forced to grow up early. I thought myself a badass woman, a hardass, a smartass. A wise owl, a survivor. And maybe I was those things. But, in truth, I was one thing more. A selfish child.

For my whole life, even these last four years, everything had been about me. I ran to save myself. I purchased Watson so I'd have a pet—yes, a pet; I couldn't deny it any longer. Someone who'd stop me getting lonely, someone who wouldn't leave *me*: a chimp with the loyalty genes of a hive-rat.

And all I'd been doing these last two days was thinking of protecting *myself* from Regis Denayer and his cabal. People who had kept me a prisoner for their own purposes, the way that I had done to Watson. Poor Watson.

But there were other people at stake. Most of them were

decent people: the medical staff, Jamie Dubois, the other restaurateurs and apparel sellers, the security guys and janitors and techs. The scrappers—well, they were mostly decent. And the ones that weren't, like Moretti, they were just twerps, not evil psycho narcissists like Scuttle. Or my father.

My long and heavy sigh felt like expelling a demon from my body.

Perhaps I had expelled the person I'd been ...

"Let's go back to the Bigmouth," I said. Toby's face softened, although there was a question in it. "We'll go through the files and check the station's schematics. Maybe that will give us an idea."

"All right," he said.

He got to his feet. I tried to do the same and fell back down. The asteroid seemed to be moving. Tilting slowly to my right as if the arti-grav was faulty. Also, the little cavern seemed to spin slowly the other way.

"One thing first," I said.

"What's that?"

"I just drank a half bottle of wine in one slam. There wouldn't happen to be any coffee in that thermos, would there?"

THERE WAS COFFEE IN THE THERMOS. IT WAS COLD AND IT WAS awful. He'd put it here four days back, he told me. I had a fresh mug from the galley when we got back to the Bigmouth. Much, much better.

At the back of the cockpit, below the bank of camera feeds, was a workstation. On it, we found schematics for The

Sandwich. The plans were a little lean; Bigmouths carried simple versions of files like these and inventory lists as basic backups in the case of a station-wide disaster. But after skimming them for ten minutes, there was enough there to prompt an idea.

"The Olive," I told my partner in *anti*-crime.

"What about it?"

"If we can get into it before Dad brings reinforcements, we might fix the FTL transmitter and get a message out-system."

"While that Scuttle guy is still shorthanded."

Yeah, there was just him and the brothers now. I winced as I flashbacked to Drew's demise. But the next flashback—Montez's murder—steeled my resolve. "Precisely. Of course, if Dad hasn't started his heist yet, the rest of the station's still on alert for us."

"But they're not expecting us."

"No, they are not." And security were effectively incapacitated.

Toby leaned in close, forcing me to shuffle sideways to his shoulder. "Two options, as I see it. Either we sneak into the Olive and one of us repairs the transmitter while the other keeps watch—" He traced a finger over the schematic I had open. "—or we break into the maintenance stores on Top Slice and steal the parts to build another one."

"We could bring them back to The Duck to build it."

He nodded. "That's my preference. Out here. Away from them."

"Do you have instructions for building a subspace transmitter from scratch?"

His expression soured. "You got instructions for fixing one?"

"Touché."

"Besides, there are maintenance techs who know how to fix it. If they're *not* fixing it, either Scuttle's guys have killed 'em or locked 'em up—or they broke the thing so bad that it can't be fixed before your Dad gets here."

My turn to nod. "If those techs *are* working on the thing, we can't exactly sneak onto the Olive without them seeing us."

"So, option two?"

"Option two. We bring it all back here."

"Excellent. Well, as excellent as a slightly less hazardous plan can be." His voice had risen in pitch.

"What are you talking about, tough guy?" I said, trying to buck him up. "You've faced hazards before. You came out here on your own to survey ... and set up picnics." The hint of a smile rippled the surface of his expression.

Moving things along, I trawled through some inventory until I had the information I needed, then turned the Angelview schematic on its axis. I zoomed in on the area of Top Slice devoted to maintenance workshops/stores/cubbies. "See this bump outside the hull?"

"Yeah."

"Man-hatch. A way for workers to climb out onto the station's skin and fix stuff. Also, a really sexist name for it."

"'Person-hatch' is too hard to say."

"Could just say 'hatch'."

"Touché."

I said, "There's a bay inside here with damaged forklifts and spare pallets. Crap like that. The compartment beyond *that* has spare parts for comms and computers."

"We wouldn't have to venture too far inside."

"Exactly. With the Bigmouth's transponder out of action,

we could creep up from the side here where there's no windows for anyone to spy us."

"Another ship would."

"If ships are still flying," I said, but I conceded the point. "We park five klicks out, then. We take a scarab, head over, clamp onto the hull ..." I slapped my e-suit, then his. "... and we enter through the hatch."

"An alarm will trigger. Won't it?"

"Damn!" He was right again. I slammed my palms down on the workstation, making him jump. It had seemed perfect. But it wasn't. It was flawed. Every stupid thing I did was flawed.

I raised my face to the ceiling, biting back on a scream. It was impossible.

How the hell did Daddy Dearest do it? How did he pull off crap like this? There must have been countless obstacles to heists over the years that he'd overcome. But he had overcome them. He had pulled off those heists. And I was his daughter. There had to be an answer and I had to be able to find it.

"I need a walk," I announced and slid down the ladder rails to the passageway below. There, I paced for several minutes, lost in my thoughts, forcing back the black clouds of despair. On maybe my fifteenth trip back up the passage, I veered through the meal room and into the galley for a bite to eat. Maybe some food would help me think. As I slathered butter on two slices of bread, I glanced out the viewport above the bench. From here, I could see one of our scarabs poking from the hull nearby.

"Moretti," I said out loud, "if only you were here, you big dumb fooz. You'd probably think of some butt-brained—"

I froze as inspiration hit me. The butter knife slipped

from my fingers, clattered onto the counter and then the floor.

"Yes," I said, then shouted, "Hell, yes!" I rushed back to the cockpit.

Toby swung the command chair to face me as I appeared above the lip of the ladderwell. "What were you shouting about?"

"The scarabs. They have a remote pilot function, right? In case someone gets into trouble and needs to be piloted out of it." Some reckless fooz like Moretti.

"Uh, right?"

"We'll use one of them as a distraction."

"...Right?"

"I'm not saying this is perfect, but hear me out. There's no way for us to get through that hatch without setting off the alarm. So, we set off the alarm. But we also set off a whole bunch of others."

"Oh-kay?"

"This hatch is north-side of Top Slice, yes? So, we remote-pilot the scarab to the *south*-side of *Bottom* Slice. And use it to open as many hatches as we can."

"Oh, right!"

"Even if Dad's here, he can't afford a dozen guys running around checking every location. They'll think it's a glitch, anyway, like perhaps their own tinkering with station systems has caused an error."

If luck is on our side.

Toby was nodding. "Yeah. Yeah, okay."

"It'll work, huh?"

"Maybe. It's not bad. Best chance we've got. Probably should open a couple on Middle Slice as well, to keep it random."

"Yes. Good thinking. But ... can those scarab arms open a hatch, do you think?"

"No worries. They can do it."

I leaned against the workstation. It really wasn't a perfect plan, but it had a solid chance if we got in and out of there quick. Or rather, if *one* of us did ... "Of course, someone needs to stay in the Bigmouth and fly the scarab."

If only we had Watson, I thought. *He's had lots of experience flying ships he isn't really in.*

Toby sat up straight and lifted his chin in an attempt at chivalry. "You stay here and I'll go steal the stuff." His body language said hero, but the tremor in his voice contradicted it.

"Nah. I'll go in." When he opened his mouth to object, I added, "You're better at flying. I was born to criminal parents: breaking and entering is in my DNA."

For the first time ever, I hoped that was true.

TWELVE

ONCE, in an old novel, I had read the phrase *his guts turned to water*. The idiom had remained with me because I hadn't understood it. Steering the scarab back toward a station with Scuttle in it, the phrase finally made sense. My tummy rumbled as I clamped the ore-collector onto the station's hull and opened the top evac hatch.

Picking my way around the outside of the scarab, I thought of Moretti scrambling around his just days ago. The memory of his nonchalance played a stark counterpoint to my obsessive caution now—I couldn't escape the fact that it was just the skin of my suit between me and the vacuum. As I rounded the scarab's front face, I swung my body a little too eagerly in reaching for the top frame. I came around hard. My visor clanked against the glass. So did one of the metal tools I'd brought along in my suit pouches, Drew's blackbeamer. I heard the visor's impact because of the atmosphere in my helmet; the muffled thud of the gun was perhaps a creation of my imagination.

I clung on tight for a moment, getting my heartrate down and swearing softly.

"What was that?" Toby said in my right ear.

"Nothing," I breathed. "Just getting my bearings."

"Are you on the station hull yet?"

At ten kays out, the Bigmouth's nose-camera hadn't the zoom to pick me out. And I was clinging on above the scarab's nose-cam.

"Almost. But don't unclamp this thing yet." It was a dumb thing to tell him, born of fear and frustration.

His reply was a tad testy. "I'm not! When you tell me you're clear—that was the signal."

"Cut the chatter," I snapped back. It wasn't for fear of our tightbeam being intercepted since it couldn't be—I needed to concentrate.

No reply from Toby, for which I was grateful.

I checked over my shoulder. The surface of the station was a little under three meters away from me. The transition from here to there was no more hazardous than anything else I'd done thus far. And yet something in my brain resisted me making it, and resisted hard.

To this point, I'd followed procedure: three points of contact with the scarab at all times, a magnetized boot and two hands, or a hand and two boots. To cross, I'd only have use of my hands as I used a grabber arm as a bridge. I pictured my legs "dangling in mid-air", a completely illogical idea and yet to a planet-born-and-bred person, a compelling one.

One of your damn boots is already dangling, I snapped at myself. Pressed against the scarab's glass, only my right boot was magnetically joined with the edging between the side and front panels.

"Do it," I hissed, then louder added, "Not you, Toby. Me. I'm crossing over."

A moment's silence while I twisted for the grabber arm, then Toby replied, "I get it. Freestyling in the void ain't no easy thing."

"Thanks, Tobe."

I had my right glove clamped onto the grabber now, my body half-turned toward it. A small jerk of my right leg would disconnect the boot from the framing. Just a tiny little tug. And I couldn't do it. My brain wouldn't send the signal —instead, it began interpreting data in unhelpful ways. Vertigo kicked in: the ore-collector was suddenly *up* and the station's surface *down*. To pull that boot free would send me falling three meters onto a solid surface pimpled with sharp things that would break my back, puncture my suit, slice open my skin.

"Tobe," I said.

"Yeah?"

"Talk to me."

"Talk? What about?"

"Anything." I squeezed my eyes closed and forced my lungs to fill with air against the constriction in my chest. "Seriously, anything."

In the small noises he made for a few seconds, I could hear him racking his brain for that *anything*. Meanwhile, my eyes remained shut as I fought with my brain to reorient, to give me back control of my limbs.

Finally, he said, "So do I call you Griff, or Shelby?'

"Griff," I replied. "Definitely Griff."

"Griff. Right. So. You called yourself Jackie Griffin. Why that?"

"Why not?" I replied and heard the curtness in my tone.

I cranked my eyes open and focused on the reflection of the station in the scarab's glass. This was a normal thing to do, I told myself, a normal thing. People went EV every day and lived to tell the tale. Keeping my boot against the scarab's frame, I readied my left hand: any second now it was going to let go and reach across my body for a new handhold. Nothing to it.

"You could have called yourself anything."

"What *should* I have called myself?" I asked him.

"I dunno. If I had a chance to start over, I'd go for something fun. Like Flash Stardrive. Or Mango Twosprings."

I laughed. My left hand detached from its mooring, sailed across my visor and latched onto the grabber arm beside my right. "Mango Twosprings. I'll consider that for the next time I change identities."

"Yeah, you should. That'd be a fleggin' rowdy name, girl."

Rowdy. Mars slang. I'd always figured Toby for a Martian.

"Rowdy's not the name of the game when you're on the run, Toby."

Clinging for dear life, I yanked my right boot free—not too hard, just enough—and my body straightened to face my bridge to the station. The universe reoriented itself in a snap, jarring me, swinging the station up from *below* to *beside* me. I felt the meal I'd eaten on the Bigmouth climbing back up my esophagus and I concentrated on keeping it down.

I can do this. I am doing this.

"Okay over there? You went quiet."

"Keep talking to me."

"All right. Back to Jackie Griffin. Tell me why that name. I mean it."

"Well," I started as my new orientation settled in place and my breakfast did too, "for one thing, it's pretty beige. Not the kind of name that gets you noticed."

"For another?"

I shifted my right hand slowly along the grabber arm. Out in front of me, the starfield had never seemed so clear. *It's beautiful*, I told myself. *Not scary, beautiful*. "Griffin is the main character's name in the *Invisible Man* novel. In the first movie they made of it, it was Jack Griffin."

"What's the Invisible Man?"

"It's a story. I just said that."

"What's it about?"

"An invisible man!" I got a fresh grip with my arms stretched wide and made ready to move again.

"You wanted to be invisible too."

"Exactly."

"So, Jackie Griffin's kind of a joke name."

"A private joke, yes." I pulled myself closer to The Sandwich, my left hand sliding along the grabber until it met the right.

"The invisible woman." Toby grunted like something had just occurred to him. "Hey, you know the way you speak has changed the last couple hours?"

"It has?" My right hand shifted along the grabber again. *Nothing to this. Almost there.*

"Truly. You used to sound like you came from Southtown. You know Southtown, right? On Theseus."

He was right: Jackie Griffin's backstory was all Southtown, the city's working-class accent and syntax a good fit with other scrappers. "And now?"

"It's more Caultan. Or maybe Grace City."

"Educated, then." My real voice, the one I'd cultivated over years of reading English Literature and watching very old versions of their adaptations.

"Mm, I'd have said snooty. But sure, *educated* works."

His tone was teasing, so I put on my best Southtown accent to call him an ass-wipe. He chuckled. My left hand had reached my right for the second time. One more of these and I'd be close enough to get both hands and both feet onto the station.

Solid ground, said the planet-born part of my mind.

"Where are you really from?"

"Everywhere and nowhere," I replied as I made the final shift across. "Most of my teenage years were spent on Foucault's Moon. But Dad dragged me around a lot." I had arrived at the end of the arm. I'd anchored the scarab beside a set of ladder rungs, so I reached for one.

"You learn to do different accents that way? Different dialects?"

"*Denke schon*," I replied in the nasally German of Centauri's Hahndorf region.

"Huh?"

"I guess so." With my right hand transitioned to the station, I got my right foot across, stamping it on top of a ladder rung.

"Oh. Is that Hungarian? My Aunt married a Hungarian guy. Nice fella. He's a cook. Have you had Hungarian pastries? Oh my god, they're so good."

Suddenly, all of me was off the ore-collector and on the station. Toby prattled on while I stopped listening. With a renewed sense of urgency, I climbed a couple of meters toward the hatchway we'd decided to breach.

"I'm clear, Toby. You can take over the scarab."

"What? Really? Good work."

I climbed higher, feeling the faint vibration of the scarab's grabber releasing. I glanced back at the big glass cube as small puffs of guidance jets pushed it away from The Sandwich.

"Griff?" Toby said.

Griff. Yeah, I really did prefer that name. "What's up?"

"There's a saying on Mars. Have a day without dust, a day without wind. You know it?"

"I've heard it. Means good luck."

"Exactly."

"Back atcha, fella," I replied in my best Southtown accent.

The scarab accelerated away and vanished around the side of The Sandwich. I'd have to trust him to get that first hatch open in the next few minutes and do it right. Trusting other people did not come easily, but what choice did I have?

The other thing I'd need to trust him with was getting the scarab back here undetected for me to get back onto when I was ready.

I groaned a little at the thought of my return climb back into it.

You've done it once. You can do it again.

When the scarab was gone, so was my only means of escape. And connection to Toby. Before the threatening wave of loneliness could crash over me, I got myself counting with my eyes squeezed shut. Once I'd counted four minutes, I climbed across to the hatch.

The wretched thing took me a good three minutes to get open, the whole time fighting my persistent anxiety along with the urge to comm Toby and see if his luck was any better. When the hatch popped open, I swung feet-first into the cramped, horizontal cylinder of a maintenance airlock. Pulling the outer flap closed, I flipped from agoraphobia to claustrophobia. With teeth grit, I recited Sherlock Holmes quotes like a mantra for minutes more until the light shifted from red to green and the inner flap clicked open. Beyond was a staging room, where I unsealed and removed my helmet and gloves. I stowed these in a technician's pigeon hole atop a sealant gun. My suit stayed on, but it was warm in the station and within the bulky getup, I was swimming in sweat. Those things are designed with tiny fans around the collar for defogging the helmet, so I switched the fans back on to keep my face cool and dry.

I peeked out into the large storage bay outside, stomach settling as I acclimatized again to gravity. It was quiet and empty of people. I listened: no alarms, no activity. Nothing to indicate Scuttle's machinations had advanced in the time I'd been gone; nothing to indicate Toby's scarab shenanigans had been noticed yet. I hoped to God they had been.

I took out Drew's weapon and ran across the storage bay, using forklifts and crates as cover. Several partitions on the far wall were open, including the one to the side room with the transmitter parts. From my position behind a pallet of forklift tines, I could see straight through it into the corridor beyond—no activity out there. That was promising.

I broke cover to cross the final stretch of open floor, glancing sideways at the other open partitions. When I looked back, I stumbled to a halt, my recent meal beginning to rise once more.

Two men in business suits were emerging from the parts room. The first was Umesh.

The second, my father.

Regis Denayer came a little closer to me than his goon. His black eyes sparkled with triumph.

"Hello, daughter," he said. "Fancy finding you in here."

THIRTEEN

DADDY'S MOUTH was a gap in his thick, graying beard, revealing milk-white and sculptured teeth. More words rumbled forth in that gate-scraping-on-concrete voice he had. The sound of it sent ice through my innards.

"You've been busy, Little Shell."

Regis was armed. His goon was armed. Crackle guns from the looks of the pistol butts poking from their hip holsters, Union police-issue stun weapons.

My hand shook as I snatched at Drew's beamer. The weapon snagged on the pouch flap. But I got it out all right, and I aimed the damn thing at him. Aimed it right at my father. I had the advantage; he hadn't so much as reached for his gun. My finger curled around the depressor, squeezing it a millimeter. My hand had lost its initial tremble, my aim was true. A few millimeters more, just a little pressure, and I could end it. End the nightmare I'd been born into. End this scourge on civilized space.

"Busy is good," he went on.

Just a few millimeters, just a few and it could be done
with.

"Busy is smart," he said.

Just a tad more pressure.

"Smart keeps you alive."

My father, Regis Denayer was evil. He was a murdering
scumbag, unworthy of this universe.

But he was my father.

My finger came off the depressor.

Drew's death had been heat-of-the-moment, and partly
accidental. But blackbeaming my father in cold blood? I
couldn't do it. Despite what I'd said about my DNA, I didn't
have his brutality.

I bared my teeth at him. My finger was off the trigger,
but I wasn't lowering my weapon, that was for sure.

"You've been busy all right," he continued, apparently
unaware of the battle fought inside me, the battle I'd lost.
"Busy, busy, busy. Causing me a lot of trouble. Stealing my
money. Disrespecting me. Me *and* the Dourani family."

I said, "How'd you know I was in here?"

He lowered his head, giving me a superior look from
beneath his brows. It was a look I'd received many times,
growing up. Many times. I hated it as much as I hated Scuttle's *isn't-this-fun* grin.

"You had two choices, girl. Hide out there and hope to
survive until we all left. Or fix the subspace and call for help.
When a Bigmouth with a dead transponder and no running
lights got sighted on our scanners—*my* ship's scanners," he
clarified, "well, it was pretty obvious which you'd chosen.
Nice sneaky entrance, by the way. I'm proud of you." He
tapped his temple. "Up here for thinking, uh? But tell me:
who's out there in that ship? Who's your accomplice? Please

tell me it's not that stinking monkey I heard you keep as a pet."

"He's not a pet; he's a person." And where *was* he, for God's sake? That was two of them now, hanging out there as loose ends, him and Toby. I hoped Dad's goons weren't closing in on the Bigmouth.

Regis snorted at what I'd said. He jerked his chin at my gun. "That piece Drew's? If you're not gonna shoot me with it, then perhaps you'd better safeguard it to my man here."

I glanced at Umesh. He looked more than a little nervous at the idea of taking it from me. Daddy had obviously ordered him to keep his weapon tucked away. But his twitching right hand said he didn't like it. He'd sidled to his left, keeping half his body behind my father's for cover.

Regis's expression hardened to match mine. "*Now*, Shelby."

Playtime was over. He'd called my bluff. Spitting out a cussword, I spun the weapon so it sat flat on my palm and held it out for Umesh. He moved toward me. When he was two meters away, I wrapped my hand around the beamer, cocked my arm and launched the thing over a couple of rows of shelving. It clanged and clattered a few seconds more before coming to rest God knew where.

Umesh swore colorfully.

Daddy caught his eye. "I'll get that. You take her to Scuttle and tell him to put her on my yacht." His head turned in the direction I'd thrown the gun. "At least Scuttle can do a job properly."

"Scuttle!" I snorted in disgust as Umesh came around behind me, a cattle dog attempting to herd a meat-beast forward. I didn't budge. "You have no idea, Dad. Scuttle's been trying to steal me away from you since I was eighteen years old!"

I don't know what I expected; it wasn't laughter. But laughter's what I got from him.

"Nice try, Little Shell. Divide and conquer, huh?" He tapped his temple again. "You might have your mother's eyes, but you sure got my smarts. Ya just don't have my experience."

"And that's it? That's all you have to say to me after all this time? 'You have my brains and your Mom's eyes' and 'Get on the ship'?"

A shrug announced he was already bored with this. Typical. Almost every conversation we'd ever had was shorter than this one had been. Regis hadn't raised me. That had been Mom's job until she died in a gang shootout when I was eleven. After that, I'd been raised by the Aunties. Then Scuttle. Or rather, I'd been *supervised* by him.

The lion-squid watching the gem-fish.

To Umesh, Regis said, "What the hack you waiting for? Get going."

Umesh put cuffs on me. This time, they weren't taking chances.

MOVING FROM THE PASSENGER LIFT ACROSS THE WAREHOUSE, I caught glimpses of scrappers picking orders. They did so under the watchful eyes of pairs of goons.

Hundreds of people had been crammed into large equipment cages: other scrappers, Concourse staff, janitors, admin workers. Jamie Dubois was in there, his forehead pressed to the cage wire. They watched as we marched past, their eyes burning with a variety of emotions: curiosity, pity, resentment, ire. Did they know who I was now? Daddy Dearest would have no reason to tell them. But if he hadn't, why the animosity from some of them, Dubois included? They couldn't seriously think I'd killed Montez.

I'm sorry, I wanted to tell them. *I'm sorry I got you into this. I'm sorry I was born.*

Scuttle awaited me in Hangar East, standing beneath the tail flukes of his Hellfish. He stood with hands in pockets, wearing his crocodile grin. One hand came out to press against his heart—or where an actual person's heart would have been, anyway.

"Every parting is a form of death, as every reunion is a type of heaven."

I forced a laugh. "Reading Shakespeare now, are we? Moved on from dirty limericks?"

"Not Shakespeare. That came out of a fortune cookie."

The only other people in East Hangar were four unhappy stevedores using hand-jacks to shift pallets of refined ore, and the armed goon watching them fumble their way to the platform lift beneath a cargo carrier.

I told Scuttle, "Can't say I like what you've done with the place."

"And I can't say I like that you've been working in a crap hole like this." He half-turned toward the work-gang visible between ships. "You know why they call them scrappers, don't you?"

"Because they mine and ship the scraps left over from when planets were made," I told him with my chin raised and my shoulders back.

He snorted without taking his eyes off the captive stevedores. "Not even close. They make rich people richer, then live off the scraps those same rich people toss them."

"I don't know who's more evil. You or Dad."

"Shelby, Shelby, Shelby. I'm trying to tell you something. You should be tossing the scraps, not eating them. This is not your place in the universe. Scarring those dainty hands. Breaking that beautiful back. Shaving off that luscious hair." He shooed Umesh away and turned the gesture into a flourish, indicating I should precede him to the Hellfire's ramp. "Shall we? Shel*by*?"

"The name," I said, "is Griff."

I hawked and spat at his feet, missing him but forcing his grin to melt into a sneer.

His hand went to the crackle gun grip poking from his belt. "Up the ramp. Now."

THE STARJUMPER HELLFISH HAS A BRIDGE THAT'S COMPARABLE in size to a Bigmouth's. However, it's a lot more comfortable. Entry is in the back, via the main passageway; no ladderwell creating a hole mid-floor; no railings to bruise your hip against. The pilot is positioned in front of two passenger seats, their chair fitted with holopad control sets in both arms. All three of Scuttle's chairs were appointed with Polluxan ridgeback leather. The manufacturers had formed the main console from dark marble, inset with brightly colored displays and a minimum of controls.

Scuttle uncuffed me at the cockpit door. There was just me and him aboard. Indicating my e-suit, he asked, "What are you wearing under that?"

"Work clothes. Coveralls." *Nothing sexy, I assure you, scumbag.*

"Good. Take it off." When I hesitated, he added, "I'm thinking of you, Little Shell. You're sweating like a cave slug. Plus, I don't want you getting ideas about finding a helmet and heading E-V."

Without comment, I unzipped, unlocked and unbuttoned the suit before sloughing it off and leaving it on the floor by the wall. It was a relief, I had to admit: the air in the narrow cruiser passageway was refreshingly cool.

Scuttle's nose wrinkled and I caught a waft of my own funk with a nose-wrinkle of my own: I'd been sweating in these coveralls a while now.

Well, good, I thought. *Smelling bad might keep the lion-squid at tentacle's length.*

It didn't. He gripped my arm and steered me into the cockpit, re-cuffing me to the arm of the leftmost passenger chair. This placed me well out of reach of the pilot's chair in which he placed himself.

As the ship powered up, Armstrong City jazz came crooning from the speakers. He lifted the cruiser from the hangar floor. It rose above the other craft there and eased out through the shield toward Regis's ship, my new prison.

As we came closer to it, I saw that Dad's yacht was one I'd never seen before. It was a beauty and it was *big*, about the size between a bigmouth and a cruise liner. Four decks beneath the squat bridge "tower". Maybe five. To run it properly would require a staff of six or seven. Painted in gold-and-pearl, it hung side-on to the station, two klicks off East Hangar, one klick past the holding freighters. He'd no doubt purchased the thing through one of his fake business fronts. You couldn't steal something like that and cruise around in it unnoticed.

"Why buy something so big?" I said.

"Why not?" Scuttle replied.

When he slowed to approach one of four docking nodes on the yacht's portside hull, I asked him, "Those freighters we passed, Regis placed armed guards on their bridge towers, right?"

Scuttle ignored me a moment, concentrating on his approach, twirling and snapping his fingers within the holofields on his chair arms. Then: "Didn't need to. I told them we had a gas contamination across the entire warehouse level and ordered them to stay where they were for at least the next eight hours."

"How do you explain the yacht to them?"

He shrugged. "What do they care about some rich man's yacht? Even when we start bringing cargo carriers out here, they won't blink an eye. Probably all drinking heavily and enjoying the downtime by now. They'll survive this fine. If they stay where they are."

"And those you rounded up on-station won't. You're going to shoot hundreds of people, aren't you? That's cold. Even for Regis."

"We're not going to shoot 'em." He spun the ship ninety degrees then leaned back as the AI took control of the retros, sidling us in to dock. "We'll blow the reactor."

"What!"

He chuckled. "If it's the freighters you're worried about, there won't be an explosion. Just a meltdown that torches the warehouse's life support and arti-grav. Anyone surviving that will get a fatal dose of rads. Won't last five minutes."

"Oh, and that's kinder?"

"Nope. Easier." The ship jolted as it came to a stop. Mating mechanisms began to bang and whirr and clunk outside the hull. "Given your tender-heartedness, I s'pose you're worried about your ape?" He came out of his seat and uncuffed me from the armrest.

I rubbed my wrist, glaring back at him without rising, hoping he didn't know that Watson had taken that scow and hoping my friend hadn't come back. But Scuttle's next words destroyed both hopes.

"I should put you out of your misery, Shel. A little while after you scarpered, the monkey brought back the garbage skiff he stole."

Oh, no.

"We found him snooping around the West Hangar."

No, no.

"Farooq caught him and I vented him."

"No!"

"Yup. West Hangar maintenance airlock. Shoulda seen the—"

I exploded from my chair, clamping my hands onto Scuttle's head before he could stop me, squeezing, shaking. He grabbed at my wrists to pry me away. I half-let him, but used the movement to rake my nails down his face before he pulled away. My nails weren't long—they couldn't be in my line of work. Nevertheless, they left three shallow scrapes on the left and four on the right, from temples to cheekbone. Blood beaded there. He tried to capture my arms but his strong grip only made it easy for me to brace against him and thrust up a knee, catching him in the groin. Hard enough to wind him and break his grip. I swung around and pushed hard toward the rear door of the cockpit, thinking there must be a weapon in the back of this ship, there had to be. I made it through the door. Stepped onto my discarded e-suit. Slipped and went down. Got up again. Two or three steps later, he hit me from behind, the heels of his hands slamming between my shoulder blades, sending me reeling. I came down on right arm and shoulder, then got my knees under me, ready to spring up. But he was on me, sprawling across me, pinning me to the sticky arti-grav matting, his minty breath in my left ear.

I screamed. I bucked. I scrambled and writhed. But I couldn't break free. I couldn't move him. My rage and panic spent themselves eventually. A sob welled up within me and I gulped it back with everything I had, awaiting whatever came next from Scuttle, steeling myself, reserving my energy for defense and defiance.

But all I got from him was a chuckle and a long sigh.

"If that's a sneak peek at what our love life could be, then Shelby Denayer, I like it. I like it very much. Just ..." A groan. "... maybe don't knee me *there* again. We're gonna have to set some boundaries."

"You killed him," I said into the floor matting. "You *killed* him. You're a monster."

Any other words were swept away on the tidal wave of grief rising from within me. I wept, ashamed to do it, but unable to stop.

I didn't let him go live his life. If I'd let him go. If I'd just let him go.

Eventually, the weeping passed into long, shuddering sobs. At some point, Scuttle had gotten off me. He slouched now at the airlock hatch, patient. I rolled onto my side and sat up to hug my knees.

When my eyes met his, he said, "Finished? Good. Daddy's ship awaits."

FOURTEEN

As soon as we boarded, I knew immediately how many crew were aboard. Three. I knew this because they were waiting for us outside the docking airlock and Scuttle yelled, "If you're all here, who's on the bridge?!"

Tails between their legs, they returned to their duties. No doubt they'd been bored, curious to see the big boss's daughter returned. I knew them by name: two older men, Davis and Yao, veterans in Dad's service; and a kid five years my junior, nicknamed Rabbit. Dumb name, indicating a soft and cute nature, which was the opposite of who he was. All of them were nasty hombres. All had murdered people.

We'd come in on C-deck. Bridge, A, B, C, D—that apparently was the designations for the different levels. Scuttle marched me up a staircase to A-deck and locked me in a cabin. It had a sanitary station, a bunk stripped bare of sheets and blankets, a narrow armchair, a bar fridge stocked with snacks and water bottles.

And a small desk placed beneath the cabin's hull window. I slumped there. Lost in despair, I stared outside. At some point—maybe an hour after I'd been locked in—the first in a slow procession of cargo carriers and scarabs began to arrive, one appearing every five or ten minutes. They would vanish beneath the yacht, where there was no doubt a receiving area in its belly. If these were piloted by warehouse staff, they were only cooperating because they believed they'd live through this, or because Dad had threatened hostages they cared about. None of them would care for me—even if they knew I was here—not if Craig or someone had told them who I was. Wouldn't take long to figure who'd brought this disaster on their heads.

The occasional appearance of these small craft continued for a long time, giving me something to focus on, something outside myself and my self-loathing.

During what was possibly my third hour of incarceration, there came a light knocking from behind me. My first thought was, naturally, that someone was at the door. But then the noise had been too soft, too tentative. I dismissed it as air passing through a water pipe in the walls, or gas in the bar fridge settling, or perhaps temperature changes in the bulkheads.

But then it came again, the same precise rhythm. And following it, a voice low and insistent.

"Griff? Griff, you in there?"

I whirled up out of my chair, casting it to the floor in my haste to reach the door.

"Toby!"

"Oh, Griff, thank God."

"What are you ...? How did you ...?"

"I used a scarab and slipped in with the others coming over here. Was easy to park. Nobody's actually manning the receiving area."

You little rebel! I thought as I pressed my face to the cool plastic and imagined him doing the same on the other side.

"How did you find me? It's not a small ship."

"Easy. I hacked an engineering station in the receiving area. First, I cycled through all the security cams. Didn't find you. If you weren't with Scuttle in the games lounge, or held on the bridge, seemed pretty obvious he had you locked up. So I had the idea to run a diagnostic on door locks. It showed only one was locked. Naturally, I—"

"Okay, okay," I laughed. "I get it. You can finish explaining how brilliant you are later. First, get me out of here."

"Easy squeezy. I tried coding a keycard while I was down—"

"Just *do* it already!" I laughed.

It was unbelievable. Pretty boy Toby Chang had snuck aboard my father's ship to get me out. To ... *rescue me*. At that last thought, I backed off a step, folding my arms across my chest, not sure how to feel about it, while Toby's keycard scraped against the other side of the door. Being rescued was not something I had ever aspired to. I was independent. I was self-reliant. I was tough ...

And when the door whisked open, I threw my arms around Toby and kissed him hard.

He broke contact, pulling from my grip.

"Gotta keep moving," he said, eyes avoiding mine.

"Just saying thank you," I mumbled and smoothed down my coveralls. It was an action of deflection; the coveralls remained as wrinkled as they had been. Once upon a time, I'd adopted a mannerism when trying to compose myself, a head toss, a flick of my long hair off my face. I hadn't done it years, for obvious reasons. I did it now; without hair, I felt like a fool, so I covered my mistake by pretending to loosen up my neck.

He said, "Of course. You're welcome. Now let's get the fleg off this ship."

I hesitated. "You said you checked the feeds?"

"Sure did."

"How long ago?"

He turned his wrist to check his seiko. "Eight minutes."

"Scuttle was where, you said?"

"Games lounge."

"Games lounge. Playing?"

"Napping, from the looks. Spread across a couch with an arm over his eyes."

"Hopefully still there. Where's that lounge?"

"B-deck."

Somewhere under our feet. Excellent. "And who was on the bridge?"

"One guy. White. Old-ish. Beard."

"That's Davis. He loves kneecapping people before shooting them in the throat. Did you see the other two?"

He gave me an alarmed look.

"Yep," I said. "There's more." Where were they? Catching zees like Scuttle? Fixing a meal? Maybe Regis had ordered them over to The Sandwich. "Was that Hellfish still docked out there?" He nodded. Didn't mean anything: Rabbit and Yao could have hitched a ride on one of the cargo carriers. "We'll have to be extra careful in case they're still onboard."

We glanced both ways along the passage. Toby said, "Those guys probably use passenger lifts. There's a goods elevator down there. It'll get us to the scarab."

"Tempting. But remember our original mission? To get a message out? This ship has a working FTL transmitter."

He groaned, but didn't argue, pointing back the other way. "Passenger elevator to the bridge. You do remember that 'Davis' guy is up there?"

"You looked at the engineering controls. Is there a way to access the transmitter from elsewhere?"

"I wasn't checking for stuff like that."

"Bigger ships have an auxiliary bridge or control room. Where's that on this one?"

"I ... wasn't checking for stuff like that."

"Your usefulness is wearing thin, mister." I said it with a wry smile he didn't return.

He jerked his head to follow him and led me to a small compartment at the end of the passage.

"Engineering station," he explained.

We squeezed inside, me watching the corridor while he accessed the small workstation.

"Okay," he said after a minute. "Scuttle and Davis are where I last marked them. The other two guys are nowhere to be seen. No remote access to the subspace transmitter, though. We need to get on that bridge." He turned to me. "How about we put you safe aboard the scarab while I blow all the air out of the ship? I can put my e-suit back on and enter once they've all suffocated."

Oh boy, I thought. His suggestion had been a little colder than I was used to with ol' Tobester. Then again, he was as desperate to survive this as I was.

"If you do that," I replied, "airwalls will kick in. They'll survive it fine."

"Damn."

"We have to go upstairs while Davis is there."

"*Damn.*"

"Which means we need weapons."

"Kitchen knives? No, the galley's on D-deck where those guys might be."

I turned my head back to the corridor. "See a janitor closet anywhere?"

"Other side of the ladderwell."

"Let's check it."

"Janitor closet? Why?"

Last I'd heard, Davis upstairs wasn't just a knee-capper or standover man; he was wanted across the Union and on Earth as chief suspect in a string of murders. Among the victims, two of his former girlfriends. Not a nice chap, ol' Davis. Not one the Universe would mind us hurting a little.

I gave Toby a nasty smile, modeled upon Scuttle's. "Janitor closets have mop handles. And janitor closets have chemicals."

I CARRIED THE CHEMICAL, A SQUIRT BOTTLE OF SIMPLE window cleaner. Toby took the mop handle.

From a nearby cabin, I took a pillow case and the cloth-belt off a guest bathrobe, knotting them around my waist. The belt would work for tying up Davis, the pillow case for gagging him.

The handle Toby took was collapsible, allowing him to wield it like a cudgel. In the passageway, he practiced a couple of swings, almost taking off my head in the process.

In answer to his guilty look, I said, "Well, at least we know you can use it."

From the engineering station, we knew the layout of the bridge tower. Seen from above, the tower was egg-shaped, with its tapered end pointing forwards toward the yacht's bow. The bridge proper took two thirds of the interior, with a service foyer outside and behind it. The foyer was partly elevator-landing-area, partly storage compartments and auxiliary consoles, a semi-circle with the flat edge forming the dividing wall with the bridge proper. Either end of that dividing wall stood open at each end to create entry/exit points. The interior of the wall contained piping/cabling conduits around a ladderwell which emerged facing into the bridge.

Since Davis might hear the elevator arrive, we took the ladder, me going first with my spray bottle hooked inside my makeshift belt. As we climbed, the occasional snatch of coarse laughter drifted down from above—the snickering and cackling of a man caught up in some entertainment. If Davis was distracting himself, all the better.

When I reached the top, I gestured for Toby to halt, then peeked carefully over the edge. The yacht's bridge had a helm station curved around the forward end. Between it and us, there was a long bench, a sofa without a back. Small drinks shelves poked from its ends. Our quarry lounged upon the bench, an empty glass beside him. He was facing the ladderwell. I winced, frozen like a Caultan grey-back caught in the hunter's spotlight. Davis chortled again—but it wasn't at me. The man's eyes were hidden behind clamp-screens, the opaque lenses fit snugly over the middle third of his face. He snorted and laughed again, squirming on his seat. Whatever he was watching, I couldn't hear it—but Davis had money, so he'd probably gotten aural implants for the entertainment's audio to feed directly to.

You're making this too easy, I thought and reached a hand down, fingers wiggling. When Toby didn't hand over the mop handle, I glowered down at him and gestured for it again. With a frown he complied. I slid it out onto the floor and climbed after it, picked it up again. With each step I took toward Davis, I fully expected him to rise and pull his weapon—he was looking right at me! But he didn't. He muttered along with some inane dialogue and giggled. I got the chemical bottle out, just in case he pulled off those clamp-screens.

And then I was standing above him with the mop handle raised. I felt a momentary return of the old squeamishness. Cracking another human being over the head with a pipe doesn't come naturally for those of us with consciences. Especially when that person is unsuspecting, oblivious.

You must, I told myself.

Davis bucked with laughter, saying, "Yeah, kick her again."

A red mist descended over me. I sent Davis the thought, *This is for every woman you ever hurt.*

I saw his gun holstered on his right hip, a pulse-pistol, police-issue.

Every man you ever kneecapped.

I saw the hairy knuckles on his right hand.

This is for Watson.

I brought the handle down as hard as I could on the back of that hand. Davis squealed and recoiled, toppling backwards from the sofa. I followed him around and swung at his forehead, but caught the other hand instead as it grabbed hold of his clamp-screens. They came off as he squealed cusswords and fluttered his injured hands in the air. His steel-grey eyes widened at me, and I squirted window cleaner into them.

The squealing continued, grew louder, Davis wriggling

onto his side and trying to rise. Out of nowhere, it seemed, Toby's boot lashed out and caught him under the chin. The thug bucked and fell again. I hit him in the back of the head with the handle. He lay still then, stunned, moaning.

"They'll hear the noise," Toby hissed, with a glance to the ladderwell.

"They won't," I told him and dropped my weapons to untie the cloth belt and pillow case from my waist. "Grab his gun."

He did. While I bound and gagged Davis.

"Is this, like, just point and shoot?" he asked.

"*If* you need to, nudge that switch on the side to release the safety."

His eyes narrowed. "You've used one?"

"As a game. Shooting targets in the forest. Clay pots and tin cans," I added, in case he thought that Regis had me shooting animals or humans or something.

He grunted.

With Davis bound, I straightened, pointing to one of the entries to the foyer. "Watch the lifts. I'll get the signal out."

He swallowed hard and did as I asked. I moved to the helm, running my hands and eyes over the various controls, trying to make sense of them. This thing wasn't built by Lockheed, as far as I could tell, the layout unlike a Bigmouth or scarab. And I'd never used anything but Lockheed's simple comms or my own slim to communicate with anyone remotely. What on Mars did an FTL comm system look like?

"Oh, crap," Toby said. He turned back to me, face pale again. "Elevator coming."

Wretched luck, I thought. We should have called it earlier and wedged it open. There were probably bridge cameras that had alerted Scuttle.

I had reached the end of the curved helm and started back the other way, trying to decipher the glyphs and icons. I called to him, "You want to swap?"

"No," he replied unhappily. "I got this."

A gunfight on a starship bridge. Sheesh. Would Scuttle fire on Toby? I glanced up at the canopy glass in front of and above me. Energy-weapons should be calibrated not to burn holes in it, I hoped. I noticed for the first time a barely perceptible shimmer across the window glass: inner shielding? Maybe Dad didn't trust the calibration on those weapons ...

I returned my attention to the boards. "Keep them pinned in the lift," I told Toby.

"Why didn't I think of that?" he shot back.

Was it this icon, I wondered, fingers hovering over a screen full of the things, a myriad of colors and shapes and scrawls. The icon in question comprised a series of expanding lines, resembling the aging wifi symbol we've been using since early 2000s. With nothing to lose, I tapped it and triggered a new menu. A messaging app with a + symbol for *new message*. "Thank God," I whispered and tapped that too.

I heard two sounds simultaneously behind me then, the bing of an elevator arrival and Toby swearing. A moment later, came the muted twang of a pulse pistol firing. I swung Toby's way. He was pressed against the dividing wall, firing around it. After a half dozen shots, he paused long enough for me to ask, "Who's out there?"

The dark-light of a blackbeamer cut a chunk from the wall above his head and lanced past to sizzle against a window's shielding. I ducked instinctively, though it had hit nowhere near me.

"Scuttle and some other guy," he replied and fired another volley. "Stuck in the lift."

"That pistol only has eighty rounds," I told him. "Conserve them."

Scuttle called to me, but I didn't catch what he said. And didn't much care. I started typing, hoping he'd stick his head out at the wrong time so Toby could punch a hole through it.

As I finished my message, things fell quiet behind me except for Davis's renewed groaning. When I signed my name, I asked Toby, "They still there?"

Something out in the foyer made him fire again. "Yep, still there."

I tapped the "TO" pane in the message, then typed *Waypoint2*, the name of the interstellar outpost closest to us. The system would do the rest, sending it to the outpost's AI who'd reroute it to the cops. With grim satisfaction, I tapped SEND and turned toward Toby.

"Messagepack's away."

"Thank God," he said, echoing my own relief.

I started across the bridge. "I'll take the gun. They won't shoot me anyway. You see if you can move us any closer to the nearest leappoint."

"Yeah, okay," he replied. He took one last peek outside then started toward me.

My peripheral vision caught movement in the ladderwell. A man appeared above the lip. Yao! His left arm rose, holding another crackle gun.

"No!" I cried with arms outstretched. "Don't!"

But he did, blue light arcing across the bridge to Toby.

Felling Toby.

FIFTEEN

Toby had been moving when Yao hit him. He sprawled forward, pistol flying free and clattering my way. He lay curled, spasming.

Yao called to his comrades in the foyer, clambering from the well with his gun hand bracing him instead of turning the weapon toward me. I scooped up Toby's and blasted the thug back into the hole he'd crawled from. I think he screamed on the way down, but that could be a trick of memory, wishful thinking.

Scuttle was at one door now, Rabbit at the other. They too held stunners, but hesitated over firing at the boss's daughter. I didn't.

They vanished before my shots smashed into the foyer side-paneling.

I heard Scuttle call out. "Okay, Shel, okay! We don't want to hurt you. We're withdrawing. All right?" His voice grew faint, giving the impression he'd retreated to the elevator and the doors had closed him in.

But my focus was on Toby.

Falling to my knees, I turned him over—or tried to. His spasming body resisted, falling back onto its side. His eyes were rolled up beneath hooded lids.

"Wake up!" I shouted at him.

Stunning, I knew, was a lottery. Sometimes it worked like it does in the streamies; sometimes it caused brain damage; sometimes the person stunned died. If he'd struck his head when he fell...

"Get *up*!"

Toby did not respond.

A white sheet dropped over me, blurring my vision. Emotion leached away. My neck seemed to lose solidity, tipping my head toward my chest. Today I'd gotten Watson killed. And the Chaplain. Had I now killed Toby too?

"You really have to stop this."

My head snapped up at the voice.

Scuttle stood above me, his gun aimed and ready. Rabbit stood there also. The younger man kicked me over. My gun hand smacked the floor hard and the gun went off. Alarms began to shrill. I'd hit somewhere on the helm.

Rabbit's next kick glanced off my hand. The pistol flew free, bouncing across the tiling. Rabbit went after it.

"Hacking *moron*!" Scuttle shouted at him while beyond the tempered windows the starfield slid upwards and to starboard. "I was gonna stun her!"

If Rabbit replied, I couldn't hear it over the screech of the alarms. He shoved both guns in the back of his pants and went to the sparking helm.

Scuttle didn't reach for me, not yet. Warily he circled me and Toby. Perhaps my expression was a murderous one, a true Denayer one, giving him pause. Perhaps he still remembered the knee to the groin. Surely, he remembered that.

"Fix that board," he shouted.

Through the window, I watched the blocky shapes of the two freighters slide by in the distance. Whatever I'd hit had sent us into a wild yaw.

Rabbit bobbed on his feet and scratched his head without touching the fizzling control panel. His mouth worked, but again, I heard nothing.

My attention split then, split between Dad's goons and Toby's shivering body as if I were two people not one. And my mind split too, part of it insisting this wasn't happening, the other part telling me to deal with it, to do something.

Scuttle continued pacing. He pointed the stunner at a flat hatch in the floor and shouted again at Rabbit. "Get in the avionics bay. Look for an override. Or a replacement module."

Nodding, Rabbit crouched and turned the locking ring in the hatch, pulled it open, slid his legs inside and lowered himself, mindful of the guns stuffed in his pants.

Maybe they'll go off, I thought. *Burn off his ass.*

I glanced aside. Davis was conscious now, aware. His eyes glared at me and then at Scuttle. He wanted freedom, but his buddies had other priorities. Outside the freighters glided by again. Faster this time, I was sure of it. And more distant. We were moving—not just laterally, but away from The Sandwich. What had I hit? An AI interface?

The fourth time the freighters flashed by—this time, mere fuzzes of color and light—the alarms cut off mid-squall. My ears rang with silence.

Stomping to the hatch, Scuttle called down, "You got control back?"

"Hell, no, I just hate that noise!"

It was Scuttle's turn to squat and dip his head, getting

eyes on Rabbit's activity. The *deal-with-it* side of my brain saw opportunity and drove me to my feet. I launched myself toward him, swung a leg, intending to kick his head clean off its perch. He saw it coming. Rising, he swatted my foot aside, sending me into a spin that mirrored the ship's.

I found myself on my butt close by the sizzling control board. I scrambled upright, swung a clumsy fist. He stepped inside the punch, hooked an arm around mine and jabbed forward with his forehead. Bright pain flared across my face. My vision sparkled with a dozen rainbow pinpricks.

It took a moment, but when I came to myself, down on my butt again, I realized he'd headbutted me. My nose throbbed. I tasted blood. As he reached for me, I spat some in his left eye. He swore and dragged me to my feet by my coveralls, then moved his grip to the collar, getting behind me. Swaying, I couldn't have attacked him if I'd tried; the blow to the face had thrown my balance off and my knees kept buckling. Any exertion would have sent me ass over tea kettle. I caught sight of the spinning starfield outside and almost puked.

Another alarm started up, different in tone and volume.

"The hell's that?" Scuttle barked.

Rabbit was climbing out of the avionics bay. For the first time, the kid looked frightened. "Impact alert! Vessel closing!"

Vessel?

It must have been one of the incoming cargo carriers. Perhaps we'd changed trajectory and were headed back toward the station. If it was one of the freighters—

Scuttle obviously had a similar thought. "Well, *get us away from it.*"

"What the fleg you think I'm trying to do?" Rabbit had

bent over the controls now, his fingers a blur as they tapped and dialed commands.

A tremor rippled through the ship. I distinctly heard a crunch. Something had hit us amidships.

"Christ!" Rabbit snapped. He checked a screen, squinting. "Okay. One of those goddamn scarabs. I think... Yeah. We're okay. No breach."

Scuttle shook his head then shook me, sending the pain in my injured nose spearing up into my skull. "Sometimes I think you're more trouble than you're worth. Rabbit, you get this goddamn ship under control. I'm taking *Griff* here down to the galley. A couple of hours inside a fridge might cool her attitude." He chuckled at his joke. But he certainly wasn't in a good humor. The way he kicked Toby's now-quiet legs on our way off the bridge demonstrated that.

I wanted to kill him for that act of disrespect.

For that and for all of this.

SIXTEEN

THE ELEVATOR RIDE down to D-deck was unpleasant. Scuttle pressed my head into the wall and held me there while we descended. My attempts to scratch at him only made him enjoy it more.

We exited into a cross-passage, then turned right into a wider one that must have run close to the portside hull.

Hull-side of the corridor lay the access-holes to a half-dozen escape pods, their hatches swung open and within for emergency entry.

Open storage compartments ran along the wall furthest from the hull. At the far end, the passage would open up into the galley area when we reached it.

I had a fleeting desire to throw myself inside the open airlock hatch we passed and vent myself to join Watson in his death—anything to get away from Scuttle and from Dad and from my would-be husband Jefferson Dourani. Anything to deny these monsters utterly and finally.

Scuttle's grip on my collar was firm. And I still wobbled as I walked. The center of my face pulsed cold-hot, cold-hot.

Electric spikes radiated outward, across to my temples, up to my forehead, down into the roof of my mouth. My vision wavered with tears. My voice sounded weird to me as I said, "None of this matters now. I got you all. I got you good."

"You got us?" he chuckled. "How's that?"

"I got a signal out. Ask Rabbit."

Scuttle laughed outright then. "First of all, Rabbit's a little busy stopping us from spinning out of control. Second of all, you didn't get a signal out."

"I sure did. And with this ship 'out of control', there's no way Dad'll get back here and get away before the Marshalls show up."

He was laughing harder now. It made me so mad, I swung an elbow. He dodged it easily, shoving me away and bouncing me off the bulkhead near the final escape pod.

The impact rang my bell, dropping me onto my haunches where I stayed, my back braced against the bulkhead to avoid passing out. When he stopped laughing, he started tutting at me.

"Quit it! What are you mocking me for?"

"I'm mocking you for your little moment of victory. The message you got out? Oh, I saw it. Got a copy right here." He eased open his suit jacket to show his slim peeking from a pocket there. "It makes fun reading. Because you, Little Shell, used an *in-system* transmitter to send it. Not the FTL one."

"What?" I tried to rise, but the pounding in my head forced me down again. "You're lying."

"I'm a killer, sure. A thief. But you know I've never been a liar."

The in-system transmitter. Oh, God.

With me in no shape to run again, he lolled against the

wall opposite me, leaning between the openings to two unlit storage holes. He savored the moment, reviving his laughter while I snarled and scowled impotently. Snarled, scowled ... and then frowned. Because something had moved in the dark compartment to his left.

What ...?

An object came sliding out from that darkness, scraping across the floor until it bumped up against my boot.

A slim.

A powered up slim with a text message on-screen.

Wiping tears of levity from his eyes, Scuttle hadn't noticed it. Until he caught me picking it up. His amusement faltered and he pushed off the wall. "Where'd you get that?"

I had to blink and squint a couple of times to get the text into focus, but when I read it, it was my turn to laugh. Or attempt to, at least.

Keeping my gaze from the hatchway beside him, I said "It's a message for you."

Meanwhile, the sender of the message moved within the unlit storeroom, their form coalescing as they crept forward and into the passage lights.

Scuttle squinted at me and at the slim, stepping closer.

I told him, "It reads, 'Maybe she didn't get a message out-system, but she did get it to me.'"

Watson was a blur as he came out of that room, leaping to grab hold of the top of the hatch-frame, swinging off it and slamming his bare feet into Scuttle's back. My father's chief goon was hurled against the bulkhead alongside me.

Trying to roll out away from him, I succeeded only in toppling. It didn't matter. By the time I'd shifted around onto hands and knees, an extremely angry chimpanzat had straddled Scuttle and was busily slapping his head repeatedly from side to side. Scuttle's stunner had tumbled free and along the corridor. His beamer must have been stuck in a pocket where he couldn't get at it.

After Watson had delivered a dozen more blows, and Scuttle had lost the ability to defend himself, I said, "Honey, maybe stop. Don't kill him yet."

Watson paused with one huge hand raised high. He stared my way with a *Why not?* expression.

"Got a better idea."

SCUTTLE'S BEAMER HAD BEEN IN ONE OF HIS JACKET POCKETS. I used it to destroy the failsafe in the airlock.

Then we waited until Scuttle came around, managing to get his head off the floor of the airlock enough to look around, get his bearings and then lock eyes with me through the hatch window. I pointed to the mess that was all that remained of the system built to stop a living person being vented. His eyes hardened into hatred rather than fear.

And there it was, clear as day, Scuttle's real feelings toward me, the *contempt* he felt for me, for every living person who wasn't him. For life itself.

I blew him a kiss. Then I pressed my palm to the waiting *release* command on the control screen my side.

Scuttle blew out into space on a cloud of condensation. The condensation morphed quickly into ice crystals, twinkling in the yacht's exteriors lights. I imagined Scuttle's body iced over pretty quickly too, but he was moving at speed, making it impossible to tell the exact moment his life ended. It didn't matter. I felt nothing as his body spun away and away, dwindling into the distance. No relief. No exultation. No guilt. Just a cool acceptance of having succeeded where my enemy had failed. My father's DNA, I guess.

I realized belatedly that the ship had stopped spinning. How else would I have been able to watch him go?

I'd also neglected to ask Watson an important question.

"Guy, how did you *get* here?"

He started to sign, realized quickly it wouldn't capture all his thoughts, and recovered his slim. He angled it as he typed so I could see.

I took the garbage scow because I was mad at you and I thought I could get out of the system. Then I realized I couldn't. So I pretended to be collecting trash from one of the freighters and I snuck aboard when they were all asleep. But when I tried to start it up, I couldn't figure out how to use the FTL. That model isn't in any of my games.

I found my jaw dropping as I read along with his typing. He really was a giant teenager, with some completely unreasonable ideas. But this teenager had some serious chutzpah.

He continued typing. *So I snuck the scow back to the West Hangar because I thought no one would be looking for me there. But everything was quiet. It was really weird. I hid because I was scared management would be after me. But I also couldn't figure out where everyone was and what was going on.*

He looked up at me. I told him, "That must've been horrible."

He nodded and turned back to the slim. *After I hid for almost an hour and didn't hear anybody, I got worried again. So I stole a scarab to go look at the outside of The Sandwich in case there'd been an explosion or something. That's when I heard their chatter on the comms. And I heard you were coming onto this yacht. I came to help.*

He stopped typing and signed, "Why is it spinning so bad?"

"It isn't, anymore."

"Why *was* it?"

I gave him a grim laugh. "I kind of shot a control panel."

His eyes widened. "Cool." Then he typed: *Anyway, did you feel how hard I banged into your hull?*

"Oh, yeah, we felt that."

That was the scarab. It's still clamped out there. I had to go EV and come through that airlock, by the way. He moved across to the room he'd been hiding in and dragged out the legs of an e-suit. "Hate these things," he signed. "They don't fit me. Very uncomfortable."

I lay a hand on his shoulder and pecked the top of furry head. "You have no idea how glad I am to see you. Scuttle—" I had to swallow to continue, to grind it out. "Scuttle shot Toby."

Frowning, Watson signed, "Toby, the drunk?"

"Toby, the hero."

He frowned deeper. "Dead?"

"God, I hope not. But listen, Scuttle also told me he killed *you*."

He blinked, then snorted. "As if he could have."

"My big, tough friend." I gathered him into a brief hug, pulling away as my bangs and bruises complained. "You ready for more action?"

"Definitely."

As I remembered Toby's body up on that bridge, my fingers tightened around the grip of Scuttle's gun. "You're not going to like what you see."

"I'll be okay. You need me."

"Yes. Yes, I do."

"Where are we going?"

"We've got a message to send. Properly this time."

WITH LITTLE FEAR OF DISCOVERY, WE HURRIED TO THE BRIDGE. Toby lay on his back—his eyes were closed and I couldn't tell if he was breathing.

Through the windows, I saw that the starfield had indeed stabilized. Rabbit was at the helm, his back to us. Davis straddled the bench sideways, his damaged hands cradled in his lap, an open water bottle clamped between his wrists. He looked up at us, blinking hard until we came into focus. His face fell.

Obviously, Rabbit had heard the elevator arrive and thought us to be Scuttle. Over his shoulder, he said, "I got it under control. Had to replace the AI module. That's what she hit. Was a flegger to get up here. Dunno why a module like that has to be so hackin' heavy. Anyway, we're turned back toward the station. I commed Regis and told him about all this. Jesus, he's not happy. Real not happy."

The two of us remained silent, waiting him out. Eventually, he turned.

When he saw the beamer in my hand, and Watson's glare, he added two words to his report: "Oh" and "Shit".

SEVENTEEN

TOBY NOW LAY where Davis had sat, stretched across the bench-couch with one arm shielding his eyes from the overhead lighting. We'd brought him water—which he hadn't touched except to swallow some aspirin we'd also found for him. He'd been reserved and non-communicative since recovering consciousness. Whether that was a symptom of stun-recovery or of adrenaline-withdrawal, I couldn't tell.

I gave him space, joining Watson at the helmpanels. While I located the correct transmitter this time, Watson put his flight simulator skills to work, turning the yacht away from The Sandwich, aiming out toward the nearest of the star system's two leappoints. We hoped to make it harder for Regis's crew to reach us with the smaller ships he had on hand. Stopping at ten thousand klicks out, we were well within range of a Bigmouth or cargo runner. But we'd see them coming in time to maneuver our faster ship out of their reach.

I'd already sent off my messagepacket to the United Nations Star Marshall Service—and received the *confirmed-*

received ping. Now it was time to use the in-system transmitter again. This time, I had a text message for dear old Dad. It read:

Regis, your darling daughter made yet another escape attempt. Don't worry. She is locked in a stateroom now. And cuffed. But this time, she managed to damage both the audiovisual comms and navigation (again). The hacking ship's moved even further away from the warehouse. I've managed to brake it, Rabbit just hasn't got it mobile yet. I'll get back to you when we can steer it back. Scuttle.

Dad's response came in under a minute. It was terse and colorful. I left it unanswered, hoping to add fuel to the fire of his rage. Also, it wasn't the kind of message Scuttle would bother replying to; he'd been immune to his boss's pissy fits for as long as I could remember. The only rational thing in Regis's message was an update: he'd chosen not to use one of the freighters, but had started loading up the three smaller FTL boats they'd brought with them.

While Watson monitored nav, sensors and comms, I crouched beside Toby.

"I got the message out right this time." I said with a self-deprecating chuckle. Toby did not react, arm still crooked over his eyes. "How you feeling?"

"Like I've been chased around a star system by criminals for a day then stunned."

I winced. "That's a bad day all right. But it's over now, our part at least."

He grunted.

"You realize when this story gets told, you'll be the hero of it?"

Another grunt.

"Toby, you could have stayed out there in the black. You

didn't have to risk your life to come help me. But you did."
Nothing from Toby. I persisted. "And because of that, I've
been able to alert the auth—."

"And if they'd shot me with a beamer? Not a stunner?
Would you have told the story of my heroism at my
funeral?"

"I ..."

Toby rolled onto his side, away from me.

"Toby, I'm sorry. About all of this."

He did not respond. I figured it was not the time to press
for forgiveness and let him be, returning to Watson's side.

"I don't think he'll be asking you out again," Watson
signed.

"Think you might be right there," I replied, also in sign.

One hour, forty minutes after I'd sent my FTL
messagepack, the comms chirped. Watson gestured that my
reply had arrived. When I tapped *receive*, a small holo
pedestal rose from the helm and a woman's face flickered to
life above it. She had severe cheekbones, dark eyes and skin,
and her hair was pulled back in almost the same style as
Scuttle's had been when I'd first seen him again.

When she spoke, her voice was deep and grave.

"Message received, Ms Denayer. My name is Deputy
Chief Marshall Sally Kain. I assure you of two things. First, a
compliment of Marshalls and Marine Corps MPs have been
dispatched to your location. Second, if this is a hoax,
consider yourself in deep, deep shit. The penalties for
lodging a false report are dire ... but I suppose that if you are
who you say you are, there's always the chance you don't
care about that and that this is some kind of distraction
while your father commits some large scale crime
elsewhere.

"However," she continued with a sigh, "*if* you're telling the truth, rest assured that help is on the way. Once our personnel have neutralized the criminal presence, we'll come for you and this Watson ... person." The pause and the flickering eyelid showed how hard it had been for her to call a chimpanzat a person. As long as her personnel didn't shoot him, I didn't care. "Please continue to maintain your distance until then and ensure the prisoners you have remain locked in the—" Kain checked something out-of-field, frowning. "—in the fridge? Hope you gave them coats. I will happily discuss witness protection with you should we catch your father. Kain out."

She flickered away, and I asked Watson, "Did that mean if they don't catch Dad, we *won't* go into Witness Protection?"

He signed, "We'll be all right. As long as we have each other's backs."

I turned to check if Kain's holo had piqued Toby's interest. He lay exactly the way he had for the past hour. I leaned my butt against the helm and caught Watson's eye.

"On the topic of having each other's backs," I said. "I haven't exactly had *yours* for a long time."

"What do you mean?" he signed.

"I mean I've *been* mean. I treated you like a child. And you just showed me that you're not. You came for me, you found a way to take Scuttle down, you set me free."

You came for me ...

It had been a while since my scalp had seen a razor now; I scratched at the sprouting stubble as I pondered Watson's rescue strategy. He'd come to my help by crashing an ore-collector into an out-of-control space yacht. And that was *after* he'd thought about hotwiring a star-freighter. Not exactly genius-level ideas. But I kept those thoughts to myself. He'd had the presence of mind when hearing Scuttle coming to wait in ambush. And he'd even sent Scuttle a zinger on his slim while doing it. Someday, someone would make a streamie about this. Or write a book ...

"Watson," I said. "When we get out of this, I want you to go chase your dream." His eyes grew round and his mouth drooped. "I mean it. You set me free, honey. Now, I'm setting you free."

He rushed me, crushed me against the helm, arms alternating between hugging me and patting my shoulders. Forgetting his own strength and weight, he was squashing me, making it hard to breathe, pressing on my bruises. But it still felt pretty nice.

Before the hugs were over, Toby got up and left the bridge.

THE MARINES AND MARSHALLS STATIONED AT WAYPOINT2 had been three hours away from our system's leappoints. It took them a further two hours of in-system travel to reach the warehouse. That meant several hours of me stalling Dad while pretending to be Scuttle. Regis's plans had started shifting again toward taking a freighter when the authorities arrived and took down his crew.

But they didn't do it without a fight.

We weren't there for the running battles on The Sandwich, of course. But we heard the details in the aftermath. There were casualties—Regis Denayer didn't go down quietly, and he had plenty of people to use as cannon fodder. The firefight on The Sandwich wounded fourteen innocent scrappers. Two admin staff died. The running hide-and-seek battles lasted three hours and cost the life of one Marshall, wounding three Marines.

Five of Dad's people were seriously wounded. Eleven died.

Five criminals made a break for the farthest of the leap-points: Dad, Umesh, Farooq, and two others I didn't know. A desperate move and ultimately futile. Not wanting to miss the chance to finally catch the most wanted crime lord in settled space, the Corporate Union sent along two Marine interdictors, positioning one at each of the leappoints. I'm still sketchy on details, but one of these caught Dad. That ship had a brig large enough for a hundred prisoners if necessary. Dad and his fellow runners were held there.

The remaining surviving crims were shipped out on the other interdictor to face court and jail in the Theseus system.

When finally, the Marshalls came for us, they ferried us to the interdictor with Dad on it. It was headed for the seat of Union government, I discovered, Grace City on Centauri. Dad's trial was too politically important to be held anywhere else.

On first contact with the two burly lawmen who boarded the yacht, my heart was in my mouth, half-expecting they'd slap cuffs on us. But the men were cordial, kind even. It seemed my brief story about being on the run from an evil father was believed.

Aboard their shuttle, they gave us a light meal and juice, treated my bruised and swollen nose, caught us up on the news of the warehouse battle. Aboard the interdictor, they handed us over to a Union Marine MP who escorted us to a well-appointed lounge. There we had more juice, coffee and a checkup from a sour-faced doctor.

The doc's tartness seemed to stem from having to see to a chimpanzat. But, though she wore those thoughts on her face, she kept them from spilling out of her mouth and I was grateful for his sake.

Once she'd declared Toby fit, he left without another word to me or to Watson.

"I think he's going to need a lot more counselling," I told Watson.

His expression said he didn't understand my point and I waved it away as unimportant.

But it wasn't unimportant. Not for Toby.

Not long after that, I felt the moment of vague disorientation announcing the shift to leapspace, something I've always thought feels a lot like déjà vu.

A half hour after *that*, Regis Denayer came into the room.

No one had warned me this would happen. I hissed and spat curses, retreating as far as I could from the door, although he was flanked by the Marshalls who'd picked us up, although his hands and feet were shackled.

"Now, now. That's no way to greet your father."

One Marshall struck him in the shoulder, knocking him a few steps into the room. "Sit," he said, indicating a chair to the side of the door. "There."

Regis stalled a moment, biting back his rage, then tried to make it look like the idea was his to perch upon that particular seat. The whole time, my father never took his eyes off me.

From his place at a viewport, Watson signed to me: "That's your father?!"

I nodded miserably.

Watson looked sad for me. His presence, his affection gave me strength.

Regis said, "Nothing but filthy language to say to your old man?"

"How about, you're the worst human being ever born? How about, you killed a whole lot of innocent people on Angelview?"

"Not me, daughter."

"Yeah. You. And hundreds of other innocent people over the years. You, and Scuttle, and Drew and... and goddamn Jefferson Dourani! You're all murdering scum."

He pursed his lips, his shackled hands raised in a gesture that said, *I know nothing about any murders.*

I wanted to break those hands. I wanted to slap him senseless, as Watson had Scuttle. I'd had the opportunity to shoot him dead—or at least to wound him—and I'd wasted it. Other lives had been lost because of that choice. In time, I thought, I might forgive myself. But I'd never forget what could have been different if I'd let myself be that bit less principled, that bit more cold-blooded ...

"You're thinking about when you held that gun on me. Aren't you?" He twisted his neck toward the Marshalls. Both stood close, eyes cold, hands folded in front. Regis asked them, "Did you know this girl pulled a gun on me earlier today? Or was it yesterday?"

"That ain't no *girl*, crapface," drawled one.

"That's the young *woman* who took you down," said the other.

"It was frightening stuff, I tell you," he continued. "If I hadn't talked her down, who knows what might have happened?"

I bristled. "Talked me down."

"And here I sit in chains while the real perpetrator of the crimes upon that station stands over there, free as a Centauran kite-bat. And just look at the violence written all over her face! Look at her! While I'm as calm and innocent as a ..." He couldn't think of a way to land that simile, so he simply added, "A terrible injustice, this."

It was no doubt true what he'd said about my face. The urge to cause him physical harm was getting stronger. And I was making no attempt to hide it. I had closed half the distance between us and my fists were clenched.

But it was a Marshall who spoke next. "Listen up, skid mark. You asked to see to your daughter to apologize to her. I don't hear an apology come out of your stinkin' mouth right now, you're going back in that holding tank."

Regis performed a textbook eyeroll and sighed. He was acting as cocky as always. But there was something missing in the body language, I noticed now. His self-assurance was more exaggerated than I remembered it. Daddy had a leak in his bravado.

"All right, all right. An apology." He cleared his throat theatrically. "Shelby—"

"Griff!"

He blinked a moment, feigning pain. "You'll always be Shelby. My Shelby. My Little Shell."

The Marshall took a step toward him. "Get on with it."

Regis shrugged. "Griff, then, whatever. I wanted to say that I never meant to cause you pain."

"Oh, brother," said I.

"I only ever wanted what was best for you. The discussions about marriage between you and that rich businessman—they were never a foregone conclusion. I wasn't forcing you. You could always have said no."

"*I did say no!*" I screamed at him. The force of it made Watson curl up against the bulkhead. Even the Marshalls went rigid.

But from Daddy Dearest, no sign he'd even heard me. "For you to run away from home was one thing. But to get mixed up with those criminals back there as a way of getting back at me—"

"That's *it*," hissed the Marshall. He didn't stoop, just grabbed hold of my father's hair and dragged him to his feet.

Regis kept talking all the way to the door. And beyond it. "I'll be out soon, Shelby. When they realize they have the wrong man. And when I do, I'll come looking for you, hoping we can patch things up—"

His gabbing was cut short by a thud and a sharp cry of pain.

The other Marshall had stayed behind. He cocked an ear toward the corridor until Regis's huffing and swearing faded along the passage. Then he turned to me and said, "Ms Griffin. You have nothing to fear from that man any longer. I can't imagine what you went through, growing up in his household. I'm guessing you'd have one hell of a story to tell if you wanted to. But the only stories we want from you will be the ones that put him away forever."

He smiled then, a grim curving of his lips and mustache that made him suddenly less imposing. "Trust me. Even without your testimony, we have enough to sink this guy into a work pit on Nereus for the rest of his natural life. Not that the UN approves of it, but after his natural lifespan is over, the Corporate Union will probably *extend* his life to see further sentence served out."

"That's ... good to hear." Was it? I guessed it was. He was my father. But he was also a narcissistic, sociopathic criminal who'd destroyed hundreds of lives. "Yeah, that's very good to hear."

I unfurled my fists, stuffed my hands deep into the jacket they'd given me. My legs had felt weak when Scuttle headbutted me, and suddenly they did again. I wobbled my way to the chair I'd been sitting in before Regis arrived.

The Marshall turned toward Watson. "We'll enter you and Mr Watson here to the Witness Protection Program to make sure none of Regis's people come after either of you."

The chimapanzat watched us with the large eyes of a wary child.

I said, "That's ... kind. But I might hit the pause button on that." The Marshall frowned at me. "There's probably something I should take care of before I disappear again. And I know Mister Watson would prefer to run his own life from now on."

Watson's expression relaxed at that. He gave me a thumbs up.

"I'll leave you two to discuss that," said the Star Marshall. He stepped to door, paused, smiled once more. "By the way, Ms Griffin. You did good here. You both did."

THERE MAY COME A DAY WHEN I RELEASE THIS STORY FOR THE eyes and ears of anyone interested.

Perhaps I'll leave instructions for that in my will.

Or perhaps I'll make it public when I'm so old as to be unafraid of imprisonment for venting a human being into space—even a nominal human being like Scuttle.

Until then, it's my story. Mine and Watson's ... and Toby's.

Whatever the case, if and when I do release it, there's something I should add. My story did not finish at the point where a UN Star Marshall gave me a verbal pat on the back.

Let's face it: no one's story ever really finishes, until the seal goes on their coffin. But there *was* one further episode from mine that I should add as a postscript here ...

EPILOGUE

ALL PEOPLE everywhere desire a comfortable status quo, a life and lifestyle that serves them well. And for some of us, we must fight for that life; for a time, we must embrace the furnace that forges us into the person who has earned it.

After the events at Angelview Station, the furnace wasn't done with me yet.

THE SPEAKER IN MY CABIN CRACKLED TO LIFE. THE DEEP female voice of a pilot followed.

"Heads up, Ms Denayer. Thirty minutes to Foucault Orbital 3."

"Thank you," I responded and the speaker fell quiet.

Pushing deeper into my cabin's armchair, I arched my back and stretched my legs, wriggling bare toes. My paperback I'd been trying to read went onto my bunk. I reached for the teacup on the sideboard but found it half-filled with cold, black tea, and picked up one of the two slims lying beside it instead. The warmth of my touch awoke the device, and displayed the last thing I'd been looking at on it. An email. *The* email.

Ms Brown. It's our pleasure to offer you a position in our inaugural English Literature program. Should you accept, orientation takes place on the 11th of Epidaurus (local calendar) or 18th of May (Earth calendar). Classes commence the following day. Please reply asap to this email & let us know whether or not you're accepting the offer. Kind regards, Suzanne McCauley, Dean, Southtown College, Theseus.

Brown. Jane Brown. As beige a name as I could imagine. For what I hoped to be my final identity.

It was no Flash Stardrive or Mango Twosprings. But it would do.

The email had been there a couple of days. It was about time I made a decision. The Dean *had* said "asap".

I hit the reply icon, typed a polite acceptance message and sent it.

Done.

I felt nothing.

For a few moments, I stared at the almost empty Inbox. The Southtown College message was the only one in there. New identity, new email account. And no friends for Jane Brown to send messages to.

I swiped that slim to *off* and tossed it onto the bunk beside the paperback. Then I picked up the other slim, my old slim, and opened its email app. Griff's slim, Griff's app, Griff's email account. Its inbox was a few pages deep, mostly filled with old employee newsletters from Bissouma-Douglas. No new messages. Nothing from Toby. Despite the four I'd sent him, and the three voicemails I'd left.

Take the hint, I told myself. *All you are to Toby Chang is a bad memory, a reminder of trauma.*

Halfway through the thought, I rose to my feet. Beside the refresher station was a little trash chute; I raised the flap, dropped the slim inside and let the flap fall back in place. A blinking icon on the wall asked me if I was sure I wanted to dispose of the item. I pressed it to send the slim hurtling into the ship's drive for utter destruction; the final traces of Jackie Griffin's identity perished with it.

"A new life awaits," I told my new slim on the bed. "Perhaps Jane Brown can figure out how to do a relationship right."

My gaze ranged across the small shelf of belongings that the Star Marshalls had allowed me to keep. The row of dog-eared paperbacks. The leather-bound copies of *Treasure Island* and *Hound of the Baskervilles*. The *Time Machine* movie poster. And the old glass-and-cardboard photo frame.

The frame no longer held HG Wells' portrait. I'd replaced that with another print, one from a Bissouma-Douglas newsletter. It showed a grinning chimpanzat in a blue **B-D** polo shirt buckling himself into the pilot chair of a satellite reclamation skiff. The caption beneath: *First day on the job.* The image was months old now.

Maybe a year or two into Jane Brown's existence, she could arrange a chance meeting somewhere with the chimpanzat in the photo.

"Fly well, ace," I told his picture. "And live free."

The wall clock told me I had twenty-three minutes until we docked: time to get a burn on.

Rising, I ran a hand through my thickening hair, long enough now to style. I checked it in the mirror. Good enough. I checked my makeup, applied an hour earlier.

Good enough. The Star Marshalls had provided me with a red-and-purple qipao. The tight-fitting dress was stiffer than I expected, due to the anti-ballistic/anti-energy armor woven in with the silk. After zipping it up, I checked that out too. Good enough. A quick spray of perfume and I was ready to leave my cabin.

A new life awaited, all right.

But first, Shelby Denayer had one last thing to do.

THE BRIDGE LEVEL OF MY FATHER'S YACHT WAS BUSY.

In the foyer outside the elevator, three female Star Marshalls checked each other's body armor. Four Centauran police blocked the bridge entry to my left, their heads bent over a large slim.

"Sniper *has* to go here," one said, stabbing it with a finger.

I took the other entry—and almost bowled into Deputy Chief Marshall Sally Kain coming out. Drawing back, the older woman gave my qipao the once-over. Noticing me, the Marshalls with the body armor did the same. Under their scrutiny, I lifted my chin and cocked a hip to accentuate my curves. If I was going to pull this off, then I had to do more than getting used to be noticed after years of hiding; I had to embrace it.

After that, I'm officially invisible again. Officially a nobody.

The women gave me approving nods and one wink before returning to their conversation.

Kain's reaction was cooler. A noncommittal twist of the mouth and a muttered "Ms Denayer."

"Deputy Chief ... Marshall," I replied. Was that how her people addressed her? Surely they didn't use the entire title.

"Need anything before we dock?" she asked.

Nervous, I fought the urge to fidget by attempting a joke. "Beer?"

One of the Marshalls snorted. Kain's face didn't so much as twitch.

"See you on the other side," she said and brushed by me on her way to the lift.

Inside the bridge proper, more Centauran police sat across the bench-sofa, hunched and quiet. Their hip holsters held ballistic handguns, automatics. One had the case for a sniper rifle beside him—I knew the shape because Scuttle had once owned one that was almost identical.

Beyond the sofas, two more Marshalls stood with the pilots controlling Regis's yacht. The same Marshalls who'd taken me off it nine months earlier. I knew their names now: Travis and Crow.

Travis had the mustache. He turned to me as I approached, gave the qipao the same once-over everyone else was giving it. He nodded in approval, the gesture a universe away from the type of leer I'd have received from Scuttle. "Dressed for success."

Crow didn't turn, leaning forward to point something out on the helmpanel to the female pilot. The *male* pilot's gaze lingered on me longer than was polite.

"Dressed to suffocate," I replied.

There was a purse on the floor below a viewport. A pretty thing, inset with pearls, dyed a shade of red that matched my dress. Travis nodded at it. "One kilogram of

Harpy Dust. And a priceless Double Eagle coin stolen from Earth's Smithsonian Museum."

"Stuff you found in Regis's bunkers?"

"Well, I didn't order them from Macy's."

I huffed a laugh.

His easy smile morphed into a frown of concern. He drew me aside to where the purse waited and dropped his voice. "I know you've been asked this before, but are you absolutely, one hundred percent sure you want to go through with this?"

The real question was, why I wasn't more nervous. Why I wasn't terrified.

I snatched up the purse and hefted it. "It's the right thing to do."

And it will bring me closure.

He nodded down at the purse. "Make sure he takes it. Make—"

"I know exactly what I have to do," I interrupted with a wry smile. "This was my idea. Remember?"

"All right then." He raised a hand and I went to shake it before noticing the object he held. The molded grey shape of a blackbeamer. "I believe you know how to use one of these."

I flashed back for a moment to using one on the airlock's failsafe, minutes before I'd vented Scuttle to space. Thankfully, someone had repaired it since then. But the memory was a reminder that I never wanted to use one again.

I kept my fingers wrapped around the purse. "I prefer a mop handle. Besides ..." My gaze dipped toward my dress. "... no pockets."

"Well. If you're sure."

"Look, Marshall Travis, I'm about to re-enter a world I

know very well." I mimicked his earlier easy smile. "You can take the girl out of the criminal underworld, but you can't take the criminal underworld out of the girl."

His turn to huff a laugh. The blackbeamer vanished into one of his own pockets. "Time to docking?" he called across to the helm.

"Nine minutes," Marshall Crow replied. He glanced my way, raised a finger to his forehead in salute and returned to watching the panels.

Foucault Orbital 3 slid into view beyond the forward canopy, a white helix against the black velvet of the void.

"Time to hit the airlock, then," Travis said.

"Yes indeed," I replied. "Time to go meet Jefferson Dourani."

<<<<>>>>

THE CUSET-DCHC UNIVERSE

There are many more stories set in this universe. To learn more about *them* and about *it*, visit

The CUSET-DCHC Universe

What follows is a short story first published in one of Poise & Pen's *ABC Anthologies*. It's very different from other things I've written, and I hope you enjoy the change of pace ... *and genre* ...

The use of the words *Natives* and *Blacks* is an attempt at historical accuracy, since those words were used and written that way at the time of this story. I hope my respect for Australia's indigenous nations shines through in this tale.

— PJA

ELFSHOT - A SHORT STORY

Being a reminiscence of William Edward Duigan,
And a true and accurate account of the happenings near
Hawkesbury,
in the Colony of New South Wales,
upon the eighteenth day of January
in the year of our Lord 1856

OUR POOR, ailing milk-cow Lisbeth lay in our high paddock, the cleared field that ringed the hilltop in the direct centre of our holding. The poor animal lolled on her side, her "bed" a wide and natural ledge in the hillside.

All thirty-three of her sister animals had gathered at the lowest point of the field, calves and mothers sequestered against the fence behind the dam we'd dug to capture water from the stream on the other side of that fence. I'd been a mere boy during that digging, all of three years old, but eager to cart dirt, to help. This was back when our cattle had numbered only four, when both Da and Ma were naught but former convicts, struggling hard to make an honest living. Now they were seen as respectable members of local society, a fact they treasured among their best accomplishments, along with raising a son destined to study the sciences.

On this day, the day that the old woman looked over our unwell beast, I was fourteen, broad-shouldered, and with a broad and curious mind that stood me in good stead to study those very sciences in future. I watched the woman keenly. She was dressed all in patches of cloth. Wool. Linen. Silk. Stitched together into blouse and skirts and gloves, covering all aspects of her skin except that creased and drooping face of hers. My parents did not know her name. To them, and to the population of farmers, traders, convicts and artisans throughout the Hawkesbury district along the Glendale River, she was known only as the old woman. (Though some called her *witch*, it must be said). Despite the fierce heat of this January late-morning, she had gathered her hair beneath a woollen bonnet. And she kept on muttering the same string of nonsense words as she worked: "Reveal thissen, small spear, if thee be 'ere within."

As she muttered her nonsense, she moved around and around Lisbeth with one gloved hand scratching at her own pointy chin, and the other feeling the animal: along her ribs, under her jaw, the length of her tail, udder, fly-ridden ears.

Once in a while, Lisbeth would let out a quiet and short-lived lowing at the old woman's ministrations, before lapsing again into silent misery. By way of contrast, the woman cooed and hummed in lively fashion as if she had pigeons and bees inside her all at once.

It was my mother who had invited her. Not my father.

Whenever her back was turned, Da would mimic her squint-eyed face and bow his back and nudge me with an elbow, making me bite down on the laughter that threatened to spill from my mouth. By the time she had completed that circuit around the ailing animal, Da would be standing straight and respectful again as if he had never made sport of her. It seemed to me each time that he could have continued mocking her with impunity since she never so much as glanced our way. In point of fact, since the moment my Ma had pressed coin into the woman's hands and bade her precede the menfolk up the hill, the woman had not once acknowledged us.

Da's discourteous impersonations were doubtless to take his mind off the heat and the boredom. Despite his constant good-humour, he had never borne colonial summers well. He was not born to it as I was. Originating in County Cork, a vivid world of green mystery to me, six months by ship had brought him to the sunburned brown and greys of the Colonies, and each summer and autumn here served him with five months of misery. Marooned once his sentence was served, without money for a passage home, he had found himself in love with another freed convict. A plot of land and grant of money from government allowed them to start their farm. And then came a child. Unlike his parents in so many ways. Born to love the heat and the washed-out colours. Me.

This was the subject of my thoughts as the woman commenced her thirteenth circuit around Lisbeth. Shaking myself from reverie, I drew breath to ask what on earth her odd behaviour was intended to achieve. My Da's hand applied a brief and warning pressure upon my arm. His small grimace and shake of the head was enough to discourage inquiry. I felt of course that such inquiry was warranted and justifiable. Yet I loved my Da, so just as the cow had lapsed back into silent misery, so did I (although I itched with impatience and boredom).

I should have had more compassion for the beast. As a young man, however, I was selfish. Just as my father was sensitive and patient.

So sensitive was he toward my situation that he began another interpretation of the woman hoping to provide a modicum of amusement. Once again, I forced back a snicker.

Then the old woman raised her voice.

· "I'm aware o' thy antics," she said, her back fully to us. "Thou be makin' skit o' me."

Since she too had come to these lands as a convict, it had not surprised me that she be English. However, her words were flavoured by an accent and dialect I had not heard before.

Caught in his transgression, my father turned a chagrined face toward me, his mouth forming a wide O of surprise.

The woman continued, "Just as I'm aware o' t'fella behind thee both."

Da and I exchanged a frown and turned.

Sure enough, a man stood a few yards behind and down-hill of us.

Trooper Enwright.

How the local constable had passed across the brown and brittle grass without alerting either of us to his presence was as much a mystery the old woman's awareness of shenanigans happening behind her back. Enwright was known locally as a big bastard. (I do hope the reader will pardon my language). To be precise, Enwright was a tall man and wide. He carried a short sabre on one hip and a revolver on the other. The latter weapon was something of a novelty at the time and my attention was instantly drawn to it. Despite the rarity and cost of revolver bullets, the trooper had something of a reputation for using them liberally, sometimes upon wildlife and sometimes upon Natives.

"Good morning," Trooper Enwright said to my Da. Me, he ignored.

He took off his dark blue cap revealing greying hair so limp with sweat that the breeze could not shift it.

Peering past him and squinting against the sun, I made out his two horses near the copse of wattle trees on the other side of the creek. His tracker Gunung was distinguishable standing with them, a musket slung on his back as he watered the animals.

The tracker was a Native, though native to lands far south of Hawkesbury and near the colony of Melbourne. Enwright, it was said, had "imported" Gunung from there, so that he had a tracker who bore no local sympathies.

Through the morning glare, I also perceived three more shapes pressed into a crouch behind the horses. Natives, like Gunung. But also not like Gunung. I could not see the chains that held them, preventing their flight back across our property and into the forests but chains there would be. The thought of them shackled like convicts made me sick to my stomach.

"Top of this good morn to you too, Mr Enwright," Da responded. "You've walked a long way up this hill, sir. We could have come down to speak with you."

"No bother, Duigan. After six hours spent on a horse, a

little walk has helped stretch my legs." His eyes shifted to the old woman. "Trouble with your animals?"

"Oh, just this one." Da took a small step sideways, blocking the trooper's view, discouraging further examination of either the cow or her arcane physician. "And how can I be of help to you, sir?"

Enwright leaned left, still interested in the woman, but he came to business smartly enough. "My tracker's horse has thrown a shoe. Probably the rider's fault and not the animal, though I can't work out how he caused it. Always buggering up something, these Blacks. No matter. I was told some years back you're a competent smith? I need a new shoe ..."

Da rubbed at the stubble across his throat and scrunched his face in thought. "Well, sir. Hm. You see, it takes some time to fire up the forge. And this is fair hot weather to be smithing. I could send Will here into town for a farrier and a loan horse."

"Damn it, man," spat the Trooper, his cursing unmindful of either me or the woman uphill of us. His face was red with more than just the sun. "It'll take the boy days to get there and back. I want to be gone by tomorrow. I'll pay you fairly. Gunung will be walking the whole way, since the wretched savage caused this predicament. But the horse is my personal property and I'll not see her lamed wandering this godless wasteland when there's a perfectly capable smith who can see to her wellbeing."

Da was already making reassuring gestures long before Enwright completed his ranting. "Not to worry, not to worry. I shall get to it right now, sir. If you'll follow me back, we'll take a look at the damage done and see if we can resmelt that shoe."

He moved down the hill and Enwright followed. "And

my own boots need some retacking, if your wife has time to see to that."

"Yes, sir."

"Also I'll need food for my tracker and me too," the trooper said. "I'll pay you."

"Of course, sir, of course, we'll find something in the larder for you. Something for those prisoners of yours too."

"No food for those bloody wretches! Bugger them!"

Enwright's swearing caused my Da to glance back toward me in embarrassment and I turned my face up toward a passing cloud, pretending I had not heard. When I looked back, they were several yards further on and neither man was talking.

"No food for his prisoners," I said and shook my head in disgust. I tried a little bad language of my own: "What a big bastard he truly is."

A tugging at my sleeve startled me and I swung around.

The woman.

I had forgotten her presence, if that can be believed. Her gaze rested, not upon my eyes as one would expect, but upon my chest. It was as if she could not raise that gaze any higher, or as if there were something inside me she could see.

In her youngish voice, the old woman said, "Elfshot."

Having never heard such a word before, and being unfamiliar with her accent, my mind made sense of her sounds by thinking she had asked me, "'Ave shot?"

"Er, no," I stammered. "No shot here. My Da's gun is down in the house." I wondered did she want us to put Lisbeth out of her misery.

She startled me again by striking my chest with the back

of her hand, and none too lightly. I staggered, taking three or four steps to find my balance on the hillside.

"Not musket shot, fool lad," she said with mouth twisted up so that her stained and rotted teeth were visible. She pronounced her word (as it turned out, her *diagnosis*) more carefully this time. "Elf-shot. *Elf*."

I frowned, not knowing what she meant. Elf seemed but one more strange word in the mouth of a woman who knew many such.

"May be I can I fix it," she continued. One gnarl-knuckled thumb and forefinger ground together as she held them to my face. "Hast tha more brass tha can give?"

By way of reply, my frown deepened.

"Fagh!" she spat when it was clear I wasn't following her meaning. She brushed by me and waddled downhill, leaning on the polished gumtree branch she used for a cane. "Owt to be gained talkin' wi' fool lads. I'll tell ee Mam." She paused a moment to get her balance before raising her stick to the sky and proclaiming a loud string of completely unintelligible words. From the bottom of the slope, the two white-skinned men turned back to regard her curiously. Enwright made some joke about her, and climbed the fence laughing loudly.

My Da, I noted, did not laugh.

I RETURNED TO THE RELATIVE COOL OF OUR HOMESTEAD AFTER an hour of chores about the farm, having eaten the rough lunch of biscuits and dried river fish my Ma had packed for me in the morning. Closing the door fast behind me to keep out windborne dust and heat and flies, I doffed my cloth cap and mopped my forehead with it. In the dimness within, and with my sight still white from the sun's glare, Ma was a soft blur at the table. From her movement, the scent of butter, and the soft smacking and squelching sounds, I could tell she was kneading dough. That seemed a fine activity to me for, being a young man, I was ever hungry, a bottomless pit for food of any kind, but especially bread.

Blinking in the gloom (Ma had only a single candle to work by and the shutters were drawn against the summer day) I made certain that the old woman was absent before venturing a question.

"What did she tell you?"

Ma sniffed. She said, "She has an answer to the problem of our cow."

"And it is?"

"None of her concern, now. Have you cleared the brushwood from the western fence line?"

"Yes, Mam. But..."

"And the fallen tree from upcreek?"

"Did that yesterday. The woman said to me something like *elf* and *shot*. She speaks like a magpie, so I've no idea what she meant."

"Now, now, young rascal. I'll not have you speaking of her like that." The words were stern, but the tone was light.

I grinned, happy to get away with the insult. "Well, then, did you understand her?"

Another sniff. Another smacking of dough on board—I could see it this time, my vision adjusting. Eventually she said, "I did."

My impatience was back, but because of my great affection for my Ma, I stowed it away deep and asked as lightly as I could, "Can you please tell *me*, then?"

"I've told your Da and that's all that matters. Now, clean those hands and you can help me here."

I made no move toward the wash basin, remaining with my back against the door. It was warmed with the sunshine from the other side. "And what did Da say?"

"Never you mind. Wash your hands."

I took three steps toward the wash basin, then stopped to rest those hands that so concerned her on the back of a chair. I tried again, "What is elfshot?"

This time the dough was flung to the board with a loud thud. "You've nothing better to do than pester me with this?"

I grinned again. "Nope."

Her scowl melted as suddenly as it had arrived. "Rascal," she whispered and plunged her fingers into the blob of dough, busying herself. "Very well. I suppose you *should* know about such things, being of Irish blood after all. Let's only hope your mind is more open on the subject than your dear father's. It seems our woman believes that the cow was hurt by... by the little folk."

It was my mother's turn to say things I couldn't understand. "*Little* people? Who are they?"

She sighed, wiped her fingers on her apron and sat upon a stool. "Pour me a water will you?" When I had done, and passed it to her, she said, "There's a good lad. Well, then. Your father and I grew up in Ireland where he was an educated man and I an educated woman. Not that this made us any richer with the English being the way they are. Poverty and restriction forced us both into acts that we regretted in more ways than just the punishment. Any way. You know the story of our deportation here. What you don't know is much of the lore of our homeland. Both of our families produced good Catholics, as I hope we have produced in you, son."

She fixed me with a stern look until I said something pious that I don't remember now.

Satisfied she went on. "But whereas his family rejected all of the old ways and the old stories out of hand, mine did not. Many a time, my *Maimeó*, my grandmother, would regale me with tales of old, and with ancient remedies for all sorts of ills. A frequent subject of our conversations were the little people. I was fascinated by them. In the old days before Christianity came, you see, before the British came too, our people believed they lived side by side with another people."

"Like we do here with the Blacks," I chimed in.

She cocked her head and rubbed dough on her chin as she thought about that. "Similar. But not the same. No, actually, not the same at all. Those poor souls."

Ma kept a small nativity figurine on the mantle. She faced briefly toward the Holy Family while crossing herself. I wasn't sure if she did it with the Enwright's wretched captives in mind or because there was something she feared that had to do with the story she was telling me. "The little folk I'm telling you of are the ones we also called fae. The English in some parts—like where *she* hails from—called them ælfe. Elves."

She sighed and drank from her cup, wiped at her mouth. Keeping my silence, I waited until she was ready. There was a gravity about her mood that fascinated me as much as the subject matter.

"The fae, the elves, are not something I particularly believe in. I mean, I did at one time. As a child. But I grew out of that belief. And upon my confirmation, well, I renounced such things. Much to my parents' relief, and my

Maimeó's irritation. And fae were something I gave not a thought to when I called on the old woman. But when I saw the state of young Lisbeth, well, my grandmother had uncanny ways for curing everything from a bad cough to a chicken's inability to lay. Except for that dreadful, *dreadful* accent she has, our old woman reminds me very much of my *Maimeó*. And it's her belief that the elves, the little folk, are behind Lisbeth's ills."

I scratched at my cheek a while as Ma emptied her cup in small sips. When she set it by the bread board, I said, "What do they look like?"

She stood with a little groan as she stretched her back then flexed her hands. "As their name suggests, they're little and they're folk." She smiled and picked up the dough. "So I'm told."

"But—"

"I'll tell you what, my son. The one with all the answers is the one who truly believes in the creatures. Why don't you go take *her* a cup of water and see if she'll fill that fine young mind of yours with more knowledge?"

I frowned a moment, thinking she wanted me to go all the way to the river, then along the local valley, past the township and finally to the hut the old woman lived in. Then it made sense to me. "Oh, she hasn't left yet? She's still here, on our farm? Why?"

Ma shrugged and slammed the dough down on the board. "Looking for herbs she thinks might give our Lisbeth a fighting chance at recovery. Take her an apple too. Make her more inclined to answer you."

I glanced at the triangle of apples piled beside the Holy Family on the mantlepiece. Reluctantly I took one. Our last three apples for the season and I'd been hoping that Ma would bake them one of these nights. Taking one meant dividing two between three people: not the kind of mathematical problem I enjoyed.

Trudging to the door, I paused with a hand on the knob as my Ma spoke one more time.

"Maybe take that back to her too. That's what she says she pulled from within Lisbeth's leg."

I followed her outstretched arm toward the rocking chair by the door. A small stone sat in the middle of the cushion. I picked it up with the hand that held no apple, opened the door and ducked outside, in my haste slamming the door and provoking a cry of annoyance from Ma.

"Sorry!" I called.

I stepped from the veranda into full sunlight. Flies swarmed me but accustomed to them, I let them roam my face and buzz about my ears.

To my left and two hundred yards away, wattle trees and a few young gums marked the line of the creek. The prisoners were visible there, slumped together in the shade. Near them, Gunung had a small campfire going and I thought he had a billy on, making tea.

To my left and from the other side of our small barn where Da had his smithy, there came the clank and bang of iron on iron.

A kookaburra cackled from somewhere along the creek.

Up on the hill, Lisbeth was vaguely distinguishable as a brown blotch of different hue to the other browns around her.

The woman was not in sight, but I would find her. By the angle of the sun, the time was around one o'clock, which allowed me plenty of daylight in which to search. I had forgotten a mug from inside, but figured she could drink

direct from the creek if she was thirsty. Just like the unfortunate Blacks had done. She was to receive one of my apples,
and she'd already cheated my Ma out of one or more coins
(or so I believed).

I held up the stone I'd taken from inside, the stone the
woman had evidently brought to my Ma for some reason.
The thing was half the length of my thumb, sparkling from
tiny crystalline fragments scattered throughout, perfectly
symmetrical, sharply pointed and smoothly polished. I
grunted in surprise as I recognised the shape from English
story books.

Very strange, I thought.

It resembled strongly an arrow head.

I SEARCHED INSIDE ALL THE FOLDS OF LAND IN OUR PROPERTY,
the dales and the scattered copses of trees and the struggling apple orchard. I even looked around the backside of
that hill and out into the bush we hadn't cleared. No sign of
the old woman.

None, that is, until I returned back around the hill and
toward the creek. I found her squatting there in imitation of
Gunung. The captives seemed to pay her no attention, their
focus uniformly upon the dirt and twigs before them. When
I saw her, I stopped in amazement, wondering how she
could have evaded me on such open, sparsely-vegetated
land and circled back to the wattle copse. And why on earth
was she consorting with Enwright's Tracker? Better to keep
her distance from anything that belonged to Enwright.

I drew nearer around the hill and saw that she had a pot
going on the fire, one she must have borrowed from Ma.

Gunung's billy was sitting in the dirt and he was sipping from a tin mug, watching her. Approaching the fence, I could hear that the Tracker was talking.

"Yeah, that's good, missus," he said as I reached the other side of the creek from them. "My mob down south, they use that stuff too, eh."

The woman nodded and stirred and said nothing in reply. Gunung chattered on about the medicinal properties of different bush plants while I navigated my way across the fence and down one creek bank, across the sluggish and shallow flow of water, and up the other side. I smelled unpleasantness, a sour stench like wet clothing left sitting too long.

When he noticed me, Gunung fell silent and dipped his head, concentrating on his tea.

I said, "Mr. Gunung, no need to stop talking on my account."

"Allgood, mister," he returned, his eyes downcast like those of the captives. "I been talkin' too much anyhow."

"My Ma said to bring you this," I said and offered the old woman the apple. Whatever she was brewing smelled so much the worse for being nearer to it, though the breeze blew it and the smoke toward the captives. The concoction looked like a broth containing leaves of some sort.

She took the apple and inspected it with a wry smile forming. "Thirty-one year ago, I were sent here for thievin' such as this. Now thee be givin' it me. Ee, but life's a funny thing."

Surprising me yet again, she tossed it to Gunung. The tracker, while appearing not pay no attention, snatched it deftly from the air.

"Quarter that," she told him. "Share it wi' thy kinfolk."

Gunung pulled his short-bladed knife from a sheath on his belt and set about complying.

I took opportunity to sneak a glance toward his "kinfolk" as she had called them: two skinny men and one skinny woman, all completely naked but for the hobbling shackles on their ankles. Immediately embarrassed and ashamed I snatched my gaze away. Ma would not approve of me seeing any woman exposed.

But though I made my eyes busy inspecting nearby blooms of wattle so starkly yellow against this sun-washed landscape, the impression of all three captives remained clear upon my mind. The contrast of black flesh against the rust-brown and dirty grey of their shackles. Their downcast eyes though large and sad, it must be said, were so very beautiful with their long thick eyelashes. Their softly featured faces seemed kind. One man, I had noticed, had bled from a forehead wound and it was now dried and attracting flies.

"What's that stuff?" I asked, returning my focus to the pot, trying to distract myself from the captives' plight.

The old woman grunted and picked up her stick. She used it to lever herself upright, waving off my offer of assistance. "Grab thee that branch there and take t'pot from t'fire."

As I moved to obey her, she shuffled close to Gunung. She spoke to the Tracker then, in laboured strains of what *I* thought of as normal English. "These three prisoners might not speak your family's language, son. But they share many things in common with you. From far south of here, you might be. They are yet your people. And you are strong, son. They need you." She startled him with a single and gentle stroke to his beardless cheek by the back of her hand. When he stared up at her frankly, breaking the taboos that many of the Natives shared about locking gazes, she said sternly, "And you do not need white men."

SHE HAD ME FOLLOW HER UP THAT HILL ONCE MORE. THE POT was heavy; my arms ached with its weight and with the awkward way I had to hold the branch under its handle. It reeked worse the longer I carried it. I had thought it broth, but it had thickened now like porridge. Like paste. When finally I was able to put it down close to Lisbeth (but far enough that she would not accidently kick it over), I gasped with relief and swung my arms about to loosen them. I fell to massaging my forearms as the old woman made busy.

She slipped off her gloves, revealing pale and much-scarred skin loose over the bones within it. She drew her wooden stirring spoon from a fold in her clothing, dipped it in the potion, sniffed it, touched it to her lips, grimaced. "Too hot yet."

The spoon dropped into the pot and the woman eased herself down on the lip of Lisbeth's resting shelf.

While I still manoeuvred my joints and muscles to ease their pain, I checked on Lisbeth (who lay still on her side). One eye turned up to me; a tear leaked from it. Her ribs rose and fell with a breath.

"Close enough to death, lad," called the old woman. "Needs to drink but can't bring hersen to walk to t'dam."

"You said she was elfshot."

"Aye."

"Well ... I mean ..."

She shushed me then, slashing her walking stick at me

through the air. I fell silent. Her head twisted toward the top of the hill and then her body followed as much as age would allow it. A few seconds later, she whispered, "Thou hear it?"

I frowned, concentrating. Did she mean the hiss of wind of grass, the buzz of the passing bee, the faint birdsong from down in the wattles?

"Not those things," she hissed. Her seeming knowledge of my thoughts caused me to flinch. She stabbed the stick toward a point forty feet up the slope. "*That*."

But I heard nothing. Nothing save the things I have already mentioned here.

"Lad, at thy age, thou should still have the ear."

"For *what*?" I asked in a quiet voice, for though I could not hear what she did, I was convinced by her manner there was something indeed to be heard.

"There," she said and pointed the stick again. "That little knoll wi t'slightly greener grass."

"What about it?"

"It's where they live."

I gawped. "The ... " I dropped my own voice to a whisper. "The little folk?"

"Aye."

I strained my eyes, seeing nothing but the *knoll* as she had called it, a lump of soil and grass, like the dozen or more similar lumps of soil and grass across the face of this hill. Nor did I hear what she heard.

"What are they singing?" I asked.

She faced forwards, but listened a while longer. "They're askin' why they were brought here so far from their home. And when finally they found a quiet place, why did 'you' follow and disturb them."

"Who's 'you'? Who followed them?"

"Thee, fool lad. Thy family."

"Oh. They sang that? They sing *English*?"

She shook her head. "Gaelic."

"You speak Gaelic?"

"I *understand* it."

"Well, what do they mean we followed them and disturbed them?

"Fagh! I can't ask them, lad. If I give sign that I see or hear them, they'll tell me nowt and likely shut their mouths. Which means thou should stop starin' their way too."

"Can you *see* them?"

"No."

"Oh. But you hear them."

"Thy curiosity gives me hope for thee. Never lose it, lad." She stretched out to pluck at grass, sniff it and crush it between her winkled fingers, allowing the breeze to carry away the remains. "Here be my best guesses on the matter. I'm guessin' they got here early in the piece. Perhaps that God-be-damnin'-it first fleet, perhaps later. They're very cross at bein' brought here. But they found a nice quiet place to settle out here until thee and thine came along. Until thy croft expanded and thy cows procreated and wandered up this hill and—" Here she poked her stick at a dried cow pat "—and shat liberally upon the very landscape where the elves like to play." She paused to knock dung from her stick.

"Play? Are they children then?" I came over to crouch beside her.

"Smartest question thee asked thus far." She reached up and patted my hand with some warmth. But clarify, she did not.

I thought I would try my hand at coarse language again. "How the hell did they get here though?"

Rather than reprimanding me for the swearing, she shrugged. "That I'd love to ken, lad," she replied. "Surely, I would. Perhaps they were investigatin' a ship that stopped at an Irish port. Perhaps they became interested in a rum keg, drank a little and slept t'journey."

We sat a while, her cocking an ear uphill, me trying in vain to hear it too. Eventually, she shook herself and gestured to the pot.

Reading her intention, I roused myself and went to lift the spoon. I carried it to her bearing a glob of the paste.

"Thee won't try it?" she asked.

I stared back aghast, uncertain as to how to decline without causing offence.

She cackled and took the spoon, stuck her tongue into the middle of the paste. "Fine, fine." She handed it back while she got herself upright. Then she dipped spoon into pot and withdrew a larger portion of the muck therein. "Carry t'pot here, lad."

I followed her to Lisbeth's hindquarters.

She tipped the muck onto a wound I couldn't see. In an official tone, she began thus: "Whether it were the ēse's pain or the shot of the ælfe or a wounding by hægtessan, then now, dear beast, I will help thee." As she spread it around the wounded area, stroking Lisbeth's belly with her free hand, she intoned, "This for thee as remedy for the pain of ēse." The spoon dipped again to the kettle and she spread more brew onto Lisbeth's thigh in an even larger circle. The cow did not complain or startle. "This for thee as remedy for the shot of ælfe." A final time, the spoon returned to the pot and she repeated her action, saying, "This for thee as remedy for the wounding by hægtessan." She indicated for me put down the kettle and she dropped the spoon into it.

Her clean hand moved to Lisbeth's head to pet her gently. "This will help thee. Run thou around this mountain top. Run around the fields. Move free. Live long. Be healthy. May the Lord help thee."

The rite complete, the old woman stooped to wipe the leftover paste from her fingers. "Thou and thine be lucky the elves wanted only to hurt thy cow and not kill her outright. However, best be thou appease the little sods. Get thee some cream or buttermilk and leave it up by t'mound there." She indicated the knoll. "All will be well by morn, lad. Mark my words." Her clean hand thumped me none to gently in the gut. "And make sure thou never ever stop listenin'."

With that, she departed our hill and our property, leaving me staring after her with a heavy, stinking kettle to clean and so very many questions in my mind.

———

MY PARENTS ALLOWED ME TO SLEEP OUTSIDE THAT NIGHT with the cow.

I wanted to observe Lisbeth's recovery, if recovery there would be. And also, it must be admitted, I wanted to see if the night's quiet would break with snatches of the little folk's song. Perhaps they would make an appearance at the dish of buttermilk I'd left by the knoll. If they were anything more than an old wive's tale. There was always the very good chance, I thought, that the old woman was a trickster, offering falsehoods and false hopes in exchange for an apple and a pair of shillings.

The lump of earth the old woman had identified as their home was three feet high and not much broader. Up close, there was no sign of its habitation by tiny people nor even by non-arcane animals like wombats. Just a heap of dirt. And for the moment, the buttermilk was serving no one besides the local population of flies and black ants.

As the sun set, Enwright rested by Gunung's fire. To my disgust—and my Ma's, I am certain—he drank steadily from a brown bottle he had pulled from his saddle bags, singing bawdy ditties. His boots were off and occasionally he would take one up to inspect the sole as if he didn't trust my mother's working. Meanwhile, his captives huddled together. Gunung was nowhere to be seen, but Enwright seemed untroubled by this; I guessed the man was collecting local food. The Natives always seemed to find things to eat where we white fellas saw nothing but trees and grasses.

With my Da's help, I set two small campfires into the hillside. Though the night was warm, there'd be cooler hours before dawn. Also there were snakes to keep away, though I rarely encountered them in the open nor up hills. After Da brought me supper, he topped up the buttermilk— to humour my Ma and me, he said—then he sat a while, entertaining me with tales of Enwright's fussiness over the horse's shoe and with news the Trooper had mentioned of the wider world. Eventually, Da retired for the night. I cracked sticks from the pile of kindling, or used them to tap rhythms against the water pot I'd kept in case the campfires spread to the grass. I hummed hymns I learned in Mass and songs of Ireland my Ma had taught me. A huge owl startled me as it flapped past in the dark. I lay on my back and counted stars. I fell asleep.

Sound woke me. An eerie intonation, carried by several voices. Upon the air I tasted Lisbeth's animal-stink and the campfires' smoke. The irregular surface of the hillside poked my spine and ribs in discomforting ways. Blinking gummy eyes, I sat up to seek the source of that compelling music.

The fae? I wondered. The elves?

But, no. The chanting came from the creek, from the deep shadow beneath the wattles.

The captives were singing.

I had not heard Natives sing before. It was, I must report, mesmerising. I confess that I could well have sat there the rest of that night listening to it. However, mere moments after it had awoken me, their vocalising was cut off sharply by a shout from Enwright. His drunken, uncouth mutterings followed for several seconds before the wattle grove lapsed again into silence.

And that was when I heard the other sound. The kind of bass-toned fluttering I might make by running a stick along fence palings. Bardi moths made such noise, whenever those huge insects came into our house attracted by light.

I turned my head ever so slightly toward the fire and my gaze caught upon Lisbeth's great eyes staring back at me. She was standing. She seemed calm. In fact, she seemed *well*. But she was not the source of that fluttering sound.

What I saw next—I will never know: was it dream, was it a trick of poor light and sleepy eyes, or did I see what my mind and memory still insist I saw?

The furiously beating wings did not belong to moths.

The beings hovered in a cluster right between the camp-fires. There were seven of them and their tiny faces had set their gazes on the wattle grove below us. Each had a body no longer than any of my fingers. And they wore clothing of sorts, its design reminiscent of nothing I had seen before or have seen since. I blinked my eyes to focus better, squinting: yes, they appeared as if they'd been enraptured by the recent Native music as I had been. I wonder now: were they hoping for its return?

And in the humming of their wings, I now heard more music, chords. And beneath it, ever so faintly, I heard singing. Their mouths moved in unison.

One of them (a female) noticed me noticing them. She flew immediately out from among her kin, a scowl defiling the innocence formerly upon her features. She said a single word I didn't know, and flew directly into my face to strike me on the nose.

I AWOKE LATER.

Dawn was a smudge in the east. One of my fires had burned out and the other was coals. I added kindling, then logs, wrapped my blanket about my shoulders and sat beside it while the fire caught.

Lisbeth was gone. A moment after I realised this, I thought I could make her out down among her herd by the fence. This made me smile.

Remembering, I searched the air around me for signs of the little folk and strained my hearing for the sound of wings. Using a stick from the fire as a torch, I went up to check the mound the woman said was theirs. It appeared as quiet and unremarkable as it had earlier. The dish of buttermilk was empty, but other creatures might have lapped that up. My only proofs of the elves' existence in that moment were: one shaky memory; the healing of our cow; and the sharp stone the old woman had given my Ma.

More than a little despondent, I returned to the campfire and lay by it, returning to a sleep troubled with dreams.

IN THE MORNING, TROOPER ENWRIGHT WAS DEAD.

He lay flat on his back, head on his saddlebag, blanket pulled up to his nose.

His horses, his man and his captives were gone. And never were they seen again.

Stories persist from this event, even today. Perhaps you, Dear Reader, have heard them?

Some believe that Gunung rebelled and murdered his master in his sleep, hit him with a rock, or stabbed him in the heart. Then he followed the other Blacks into the night, carrying away the white man's goods. Those who believe this take no stock in the facts: his horses and their saddles were taken, but the rest of his goods remained, including his revolver; no wound was found on Enwright's head, no stab wound on his body and there was no indication around his neck of stranglement.

"Then," others claim, "he was smothered." And yet the ground around him was undisturbed as would be expected in a struggle, since no man would accept suffocation without a fight.

Others say that Gunung poisoned Enwright's tea. But that belies the common knowledge that Enwright (fearful of such treatment from the Blacks he so despised) always had his Tracker drink from the same billy a full half hour before he would touch it himself.

Of course these stories persist. Because it is only now that I inform the world of the truth, of what I found on (or rather *in*) the Trooper's body.

Under pretence of checking him for snake bite, I did what I had seen the old woman do with Lisbeth: I ran my hands along the exposed areas of the man's skin. Until my hand caught upon a lump, so small I almost missed it. Something inorganic and tiny protruded from the flesh, just below the collar of his shirt and along the triangular muscle of his shoulder. Between my fingernails, I seized it. Tugging brought it loose. I turned it over in my hand. Not much larger than a splinter someone might get by bumping against a fence: but this was stone. The size of the moon on my smallest finger's nail.

And perfectly shaped.

Like an arrow head.

ACKNOWLEDGMENTS

Gratitude is due ...

My thanks to Liz, Dave and Janine who kindly pre-read SCRAPPER for me, suggesting improvements and hunting down errors.

Any errors remaining are my bad.

Thanks also to Ronnie Jensen for the kick ass cover.

EXCERPT FROM THE NOVEL "THIRD CONTACT"

The fireteam's formation around the door was the same as the one they'd adopted when boarding the pirate corvette. Chipper and Stines stood behind a kneeling Ana and Hecate respectively, weapons ready, riding out the mild bumps as the yacht settled to the hangar floor. In contrast, the Tluaan warrior Vazak rested against the bulkhead opposite the hatch, one hand on her shoulder-holster, the other on her hip, the very picture of unfazed.

Chipper swallowed against the lump in his throat, but couldn't budge it. His eyes fell to the selector switch on the side of his PR19: it was set to *AP*, "anti-personnel" being the clean way of describing a lethal setting.

Do what you have to. Do what you must. You're a soldier, damn it.

He raised his chin and the lump in his throat dissolved as acceptance flooded through him. A click announced the hatch lock disengaging. The rustle of cloth and creak of gloves announced the fireteam's grips tightening on weapons. Chipper heard Wepps coming up beside him from the cockpit.

"Five bogeys sighted," the team leader said. "They fled down a passage to your ten o'clock."

The hatch slid open, the ramp already engaging, lowering from the ship's hull before rolling out like a rug. *Unlike* a rug, it hardened immediately into a stable surface as it touched the hangar's concrete floor. Without hostile contacts out there, Ana and Hecate shot to their feet and charged down, the male Peacers at their heels. Ana curved left toward the cockpit as Hecate and Stines veered right to the tail. Perched atop legs two meters high, there was space beneath the yacht's belly for Ana and Wepps to cut under it rather than around. They didn't stoop; Chipper had to. He glanced behind him, to where Vazak pounded out into the middle of empty space, without cover, turning in circles, seeking an enemy.

Cripes alive!

He faced forward again, putting her out of mind. His nostrils now prickled from the smell and bite of petrochemicals and concrete dust. To his right, patches of sunlight breaking through the hangar's opaque window-panels formed warm yellow rectangles across the floor. That was the only color here apart from the paint job on the yacht: the hangar design was utilitarian, greys upon greys. No other vehicles were in here, but a network of gantries, small derricks and catwalks laced the perimeter and beams crisscrossed the ceiling. Now that he looked more carefully, the roof seemed to be shifting a little in the outside breeze. Some kind of shade cloth? A kind of insulating fabric, more likely: it was cool in here while the glare beyond the hangar entrance hinted at a very hot day.

Through the stink of chemical and construct, Chipper could discern something else now, a native musk left by the beings that had been working here perhaps. Or by something in the atmosphere. He thanked God for the nanite-inoculations he'd received against germs ...

Wepps pointed to a doorway eighty meters off the yacht's nose. Ana already had her rifle angled that way; Chipper did the same.

"Straight through there," Wepps said as Hecate came around from their left. Stines had stayed by the tail with an eye on the open hangar entrance. "Tluaan intel says the data center's where the building's four wings meet." He pointed at Hecate. "You're on point, then me, Ana, Stines."

"What about her?" Ana asked, jerking her shoulder at Vazak. The huge warrior was pacing now, nose in the air.

"She's meant to stick with me," Wepps sighed. "I'll guess we'll see about that."

"What about *me*?" Chipper asked.

"Watch the ship," Wepps said simply. "Go, Hecate."

Hecate bounded away at a sprint. A second later, Ana did too, but Chipper snared Wepps's armor to hold him place as Stines raced over and past them.

"Sergeant, if it's what I said about not capturing an enemy leader—"

Wepps's surprised expression softened. "It's not, Chip. I need someone here who can actually do what they're told and keep this ship intact for when we get back. I'd like to leave here when I need to."

"Right, Sergeant," Chipper replied, caught between relief and the shame of feeling relieved. He let Wepps go and the sergeant cuffed him affectionately before he too raced away.

Hecate was almost at the door before Vazak seemed to notice and follow. Despite her bulk, the Tlaa was *fast*, those long legs eating up the space at twice a human's speed.

"You need me?" a voice asked from behind him. Piers. Halfway down the ramp and ashen-faced, but steeled for the worst.

"Cockpit," Chipper told him. "Keep the engines warm. Be ready to go at a moment's notice."

With a nod, Piers scampered back inside.

Chipper glanced down at the stubby grenade launcher under his PR19's muzzle. *Hope you guys don't need this.* He took a knee under the vessel and kept his head on a swivel, watching both the hangar entrance and the door—the door through which his team were fast disappearing.

A gaggle of Tluaanto awaited them, one hundred meters along the corridor. They reminded Ana of gawkers at a road-side accident. Ten of them, all unarmed, none anywhere near Vazak's size. From a hundred meters away—most of the way to the building's hub—they stared at the alien inter-lopers coming through their door.

What is this, show time at the zoo? Ana wondered.

Without warning, Hecate burst-fired from beside her. Ana flinched. The EM rounds slammed against the ceiling above the crowd, showering them with fragments and dust and sending them packing.

Passing her human teammates, Vazak jogged ahead, her pistol out of its holster. She squeezed off a shot of her own, the energy bolt sizzling just over the heads of the fleeing. The group broke into two, vanishing behind side doors. As the fireteam jogged after her, Vazak looked over her shoulder and called, "Fun!"

"Christ," Stines grumbled to Hecate. "She's crazier'n you are!"

Hecate sent him a crass gesture.

Wepps snapped, "Secure those doors," indicating the ones the civilians had gone through. The cutting lasers carried by Hecate and Stines were also good for melting metal, melding doorframes to doors. When they reached the rooms the Tluaanto personnel had gone into, Stines stayed behind, putting his cutter to work. The others continued on, Wepps and Hecate checking the other side rooms as Ana and Vazak kept on at a walk toward the open space another hundred meters further. The data center. Despite his orders to them to use lethal force, when Ana heard Wepps's weapon go off twice behind her, the sound was that of stun bolts.

Can't bring himself to kill non-combatants, she thought. *Well, fair play to you, Sergeant. That's exactly why I wanna join you Confeds.*

"Seal this one too," he shouted back to Stines.

Nearing the open area mid-building, Ana saw movement in there. More civilians? Or—

Her instincts saved her life. A shaggy head and broad shoulders appeared above a work station just inside the main chamber; Ana ducked right and into the final office doorway of the corridor. An energy bolt crackled past her left shoulder. Another hit the wall above the doorframe, forcing Ana to jiggle at the handle until it opened. Outside, Wepps and Hecate had gone to ground, Hecate pulling something from a hip pouch. Vazak appeared mid-corridor right outside the room Ana was in, firing from the hip. She heard an agonized shriek from the data center and Vazak sauntered into the room with her to take cover at the door, unfazed.

Making eye contact, Ana said, "Still fun?"

"Fun," the big Tlaa confirmed.

"Roachbot active," Hecate called out in the hall.

Ana risked a peek. From a prone position, Hecate had the tiny controller for the bot in her hands while the robot scuttled along the hallway floor at great speed.

"Careful of collaterals," Wepps called to her. "We want those leaders if they're there."

"Trust me," Hecate replied. "Dialing it down."

Several more energy bolts flashed past, forcing Ana to retreat. Vazak returned fire, but without a resulting cry of pain this time.

"Two bogeys only, eleven o'clock," Hecate called and then blue-white light flashed once followed by a thick *whump* of sound. She'd used the flashboom setting on the bot, Ana realized, rather than H.E. A half second later she also realized that her crew were moving. She followed after Vazak as fast as she could, but the Tlaa quickly overtook Hecate and Wepps, entering the chamber ahead of them and to the left of the doorway. The warrior was one meter inside—with Wepps coming up mid-corridor and Hecate far-right—when something huge dropped on her from the ceiling and she rolled sideways and out of Ana's view. Wepps and Hecate swore, Wepps with rifle high and sweeping the roof, while Hecate's swept the maze of work stations around the room, favoring the left of the chamber's midpoint. Satisfied there was no further threat from above, Wepps leaped onto a console and fired repeatedly at the point Ana figured the flashboomed hostiles were.

"Two down," he called and jumped to the next console, tracking his rifle left for new threats while Hecate focused right.

Reaching the entrance to the chamber, Ana threw herself on the floor. All of the desks appeared to be standing up off the floor with a meter of space beneath them—this allowed her to check the room from a prone position. A quick glance to her left revealed Vazak grappling with a warrior of similar size, with bushier head-fur and more formal clothes. They scuttled around on one hand and two knees, both with knives drawn and teeth bared. They came together in a tangle as Ana forced her focus ahead of her.

There!

"Contact forward!" she yelled. "Mid-room. Four, maybe five bogeys. Could be civs." The knot of Tluaanto were bowed low, with knees, hands and heads all touching the floor. None appeared as big as the warriors she'd seen so far.

"Got 'em!" Wepps yelled from above and forward. "Ana, you're free to move. Hecate—"

"Still clearing," the Tactical called back.

Ana got up and slipped down an aisle way between desks, bringing her close to the sergeant's position as he hopped to the floor. She smelled charred flesh and fabric: over to the left, two enemy warriors were down with smoking holes in their torsos and heads.

"Hack it, I missed all the action!" Stines whined, entering the chamber late. He pulled up short, captivated by the two grappling warriors.

"They're yours to watch," Wepps told him. When he noticed Ana trying to pick out the council members from the five Tluaanto cowering on their knees mid-room, he whistled at her. "Forget them." He stabbed a finger at a nearby data terminal as he closed on the frightened huddle of nonhumans.

"Right," she said and bent over the work station. She slipped her folding keypad and smartwire from a vest pocket and got to work, recognizing the data port she'd been shown back on *Assured*. The port was a configuration of three slim holes arranged in a tight triangle. Squeezing the smartwire's end to activate it, she pressed it against the metal between the holes. While she caught her breath, the wire's end parted into tiny filaments that snaked their way against and into the input apertures. She fit the other end of the smartwire into the keypad.

"Clear!" Hecate called.

With one hand training his rifle on the group of cowering Tluaanto, Wepps waved the other at the door on the far side of the chamber. "That's front door. Hecate, that's yours to watch." He stabbed a finger back the way they'd come. "That's back door. Stines, that's yours—and keep an eye on … them," he added, meaning the warriors down behind the bank of work stations.

"Bloody oath, I will," Stines replied.

Ana checked the keypad, waiting for the green light and bright alert tone that would signal contact had been established. It wasn't coming fast and she found herself bobbing up and down on the balls of her feet. "Come on, *porquería*, come on!"

Ahead of her, Wepps pulled items from the largest pouch on his vest. Three cakes of high explosive. Then the detonator.

Once the virus was on its way, Wepps was going to turn this place to atoms.

Yes! she thought as the keypad bleeped confirmation of a

connection. Suddenly, nothing mattered so much to her as uploading the data virus and getting the hack out of here. She hoped Piers still had the yacht engines running. She hoped Chipper wasn't facing any contacts back there—

Joyful whooping from Stines turned Ana's head: Vazak had risen from behind the bank of desks, wiping dark blood from her knife onto her suit leg. There didn't appear to be any tears in that suit. From his position covering the entryway, Stines flipped the Tlaa a thumbs up. She ignored it, vaulting over consoles to get to Ana's station faster. Although Ana knew Vazak was on her side, watching that mighty body approaching at full steam, her ape-cat face flushed and her throat fur dark, with that huge blade drawn —holy Christ, it was *scary*.

At Ana's side, Vazak considered the ovular monitor screen at the back of the work station. Ana clipped a data-wafer to the keypad—the wafer containing the mutated virus—and started typing. All of this had to be by memory and with a precise touch since none of the right-to-left gibberish running across the alien monitor screen made any sense to her. It didn't need to, she reminded herself. She'd programmed the virus with a little help from that gambling addict Sintopas and one of the Orbital's crew; it was solid. As long as her typing *was* accurate, the program she unleashed would bridge human and Tluaan systems to send that data-virus racing out into Domain Surface networks at lightspeed.

Vazak grunted something and it took Ana a few moments to recognize it as the English word *Good*. The warrior was already moving away and toward the seated captives before Ana could respond.

Vazak pointed at one of the trembling Tluaanto—Ana

couldn't tell their gender at a glance, especially not when distracted and awaiting a confirmation bleep from her keypad. *Come on, come on*, she thought. Vazak barked commands at the Tluaan individual—straightening, Ana noticed that this one wore a short robe over the normal Tluaan tunic and trousers, a garment with silver embossing along the sleeves and hem. After a moment, the individual crawled along the floor until they were two metres from the rest of their group. They glared back at Vazak, covering their fear with an exaggerated hauteur.

Vazak said to Wepps, "Con-sill."

"Copy," Wepps replied. He raised his voice. "We're not taking these other four. Or incinerating them. Vazak, tell them to run." He mimed it with his fingers and pointed to the front door.

Vazak frowned a little and watched his lips as he repeated the words.

Her expression cleared. "Run. Yes." She turned to the four civilians and snarled three syllables at them. Nothing happened except that they drew tighter in on themselves. Vazak drew a deep breath. This time she roared the phrase at them. And this time, they didn't hesitate, rising as one and bolting hard toward the entry Hecate was guarding. The Tactical slapped her rifle barrel against the backside of the last one leaving and cackled.

Wepps approached the last enemy individual—the Surface council member—waving them to their feet. They complied—grudgingly. Immediately, Vazak stepped in and scooped the individual onto her shoulder, the way she had with Hecate. Then she retreated around the desks at a jog.

Ana's comms crackled—they'd been able to rig them to operate in a closed system away from *Assured*. They could communicate amongst themselves but not with their capital ship.

"Fireteam, this is Chipper. Pilot marks three aircraft inbound fast and low from the north. Devilfly is distracted and can't engage."

Wepps hit *transmit* button. "Close?"

"Very."

"Troop carriers? Bombers?"

"Can't be certain."

"Copy." Wepps whistled Hecate and gestured for her to come back. He hit the detonator timer and set out after Vazak. "Two minutes till boom-boom, boys and girls, let's frog it!" He slapped his comms again. "Returning hot, Chipper. Vazak has one enemy prisoner."

Ana squeezed the smartwire, telling it to withdraw.

Chipper's voice crackled through their comms again. "Radar indicates first enemy aircraft has landed, north end of compound. First enemy aircraft has landed."

Ana tugged out the data wafer and pocketed it, folding the keyboard as Hecate arrived at her side. She gave the wire a tug, but it wouldn't detach. What was taking it so long?

"The man said boom-boom," Hecate told her. "You know boom-boom?"

"Go if you have to. I'll be done in a sec."

"Leave it!"

"Can't! Captain doesn't want traces of human tech left here."

"Screw him!"

Ana wondered if Hecate would have said that aloud if her ECF had been sending to *Assured.*

Hecate continued, "The tech's about to get evaporated. Let's *go.*"

"They're orders. Just leave. I'm almost d—"

A deep-throated shout from the direction of the "front door" sucked the breath out of Ana's lungs. Warriors? How the hell had they—?

She flashed back to a memory of Vazak sprinting through the hangar and overtaking her.

"Shit."

She trained her rifle on the door a split second after Hecate did. The very next second, two enormous Tluaanto came barreling through it. They wore clothing closer to human combat fatigues than to Vazak's bodysuit. Their head-fur was shaggier than hers. And they were bigger. Both carried long knives, their rifles slung. Seeing the humans, they ululated and cut toward them, hurdling the first desk in their way.

Ana and Hecate fired simultaneously, a sustained volley that blew both hostiles off their feet and back onto the desk.

"Now will you go?" Hecate asked her, turning her head for a second.

In the second that followed, an energy bolt whipped by, centimeters overhead. Ana had the impression of three or four more warriors crowding the doorway before she dropped into cover.

"Holy mother!" Hecate hissed, collapsing next to Ana.

"You hit?"

"Nah, just pissed off."

"Bad timing, huh?"

"Damn right." A barrage of energy bolts swept overhead, turning patches of the next desks past them into molten slag. "What now?"

Ana's keypad and smartwire were still up on the desk. She wished she'd listened to Hecate and left them thirty seconds ago—she was going to have to anyway. She jerked her chin at the "back door".

"Head for the corridor. I'll cover you. Then you cover me while I catch up."

"So they can hit me while you hit them?" Hecate sneered.

"God! I'm trusting *you* not to run and leave me here!"

"It's a dumbass idea, whoever goes first."

Both women recoiled when fresh fire pounded the back of the desk they'd sheltered behind.

"That's gonna burn through real soon," Hecate said.

Ana pulled a grenade from a vest pouch. Hecate nodded and followed suit. They scooted to opposite ends of their cover, coming around into a crouch to face it. Ana slung the rifle over her back and pulled her sidearm—the Xerxian 12-mm felt a lot more comfortable than the Confed rifles, and it would be easier to fire blind over a desk. There came a temporary lull in the shooting, and with it the scuff of footsteps as hostiles repositioned themselves.

"Me first," Ana said. Hooking her forearm over the desk, she fired four wild shots. When return-fire hammered home near her, Hecate lobbed her grenade then ducked back. Ana quickly twisted the top of her grenade and depressed the timer. Enemy fire swung Hecate's way, allowing Ana to lob her grenade too, careful to send it far past Wepps's charges. The two women jammed hands over ears and opened their jaws wide against the pressure wave to come.

The twin explosions shook the floor and rattled the desk. Rubble peppered the room and smoke boiled quickly up toward the high ceiling.

"*Now* I'll go first!" Hecate said and launched herself in the direction of the back door.

Ana popped up, handgun ready ... But there was zero enemy contact. And judging by the mess they'd caused, there wouldn't be. Her anxious gaze fell to Wepps's explosives, sitting undamaged where he'd placed them. How much time had elapsed?

Ana turned and sprinted after Hecate. The other Tactical had paused by the door to offer cover if needed, so Ana passed her easily and heard her fall into step a few meters behind.

They were fifty or meters out of the data center when the charges ignited.

The resulting pressure wave threw them off their feet. Ana tucked herself into a roll as she landed, coming to rest face up and in perfect position to watch the network of cracks race along the ceiling above her.

"Shit!" she cried and hunkered up tight again, arms over her head as the roof caved in.

Third Contact: out now!
Find out about it and more Peter J Aldin books at *http://petealdin.com/library/* or on https://www.amazon.com/Pete-Aldin/e/B06WRNVHJP.

www.ingramcontent.com/pod-product-compliance
Lightning Source LLC
Chambersburg PA
CBHW030307200626
46816CB00002BA/806